DISPATCHED

BY
KANDEE ANN KAHN

ISBN: 1453801391
ISBN-13: 9781453801390

Tonight was the night. They had planned it so nothing would go wrong. So why was she so scared and nervous? She looked around at the Reno Police Dispatch Center. She saw Caryn sitting at the phone console answering a 911 call. She saw Lynda sitting at the fire department console dispatching a medical emergency to Reno Engine 2. She observed Mike sitting at the county console. He was reading a book in between dispatching calls to the deputies working graveyard shift for Washoe County Sheriffs Dept. She wasn't too busy working at the police console, working the police radio for the Reno Police Department. Thank goodness she wasn't busy. No one was to be on any calls between the hours of 3 & 4 A.M. She had been employed with the Reno Police Department communications center for 9 1/2 months.

Carla was twenty two years old. She had led a sheltered life, being home schooled all her life. She was an only child. Her parents were concerned for her, since she was very immature. But, once Carla turned eighteen, she moved out of the house. Carla decided she was going to have the fun she missed, while she had been living with her parents. Carla's first job was answering phones for a busy attorney's office. Carla thought she would meet a handsome rich attorney. They would fall in love and he would spoil her rotten.

He would buy her everything, and anything, her "little heart" desired.

Instead, Carla worked long hours, and never got the attention, or recognition, she craved. That is, not until Tommy came along. Carla met Tommy when she stopped at her favorite coffee shop, before she went home. Tommy swore to Carla that it was love at first sight, when Carla asked for a mocha latte. Carla felt that Tommy was everything she had been looking for. Tommy was tall, very good looking, had a sweet smile, and he adored Carla. The only problem with Tommy was that he did not have any money.

Tommy was living with his older brother Gary. Gary scared Carla, but Tommy told her Gary was really a nice guy. He just looked mad all the time. Tommy told Carla that Gary was concerned about their financial situation. Carla could understand that. Carla was concerned about Tommy's lack of finances too.

Before Carla had met Tommy, Carla had applied for a job as an emergency dispatcher with the City of Reno. Just a couple of weeks after Carla started dating Tommy, she got a letter in the mail telling her she was hired. Carla was excited because she would be making more money.

Carla attended a dispatch academy, which was held in the dispatch center. Carla was disappointed that it was in the basement of the fire station. But, Carla liked to see the firemen when she came to class everyday. Carla's academy class had four other people in it. Carla did not like anyone there, because Carla knew she was better than they were, but she was not getting the recognition she deserved. After all, she was the smartest person who had ever attended the academy. And she was pretty too. Tommy always told her she was smart and pretty. Carla liked the fact that she had week-ends off. Tommy always took her to dinner and a movie Saturday night. Sunday was the only day they had off together. Tommy worked six days a week.

Carla complained to Tommy that she hated being in the basement of a building all day. She started calling it a dungeon. Tommy told her if he had enough money, he would marry her and she would never have to work again. Carla would sigh and say "oh Tommy, I wish that would happen tomorrow." Tommy would look forlorn and say "me too."

One day Carla and the other dispatchers all got sick at work. Carla was told later that someone had parked their diesel truck outside by "that air vent." The driver had left the truck running while he ran inside. When Carla called Tommy later that night she told him what had happened. Tommy mentioned to Gary why Carla could not go out on their regular Saturday night date. Carla never thought Tommy would tell Gary about the air vent.

Gary came up with the plan. Gary told Tommy, who told Carla, that none of them would ever have to work again. They would never have to worry about finances. Gary had the perfect plan. Gary, Tommy, and Carla just had to wait for the perfect time.

It took that long to plan for this day. It also took this week, out of the entire year, for just this moment. "Kool Klassic Nights." The biggest event of the year. It occurred in Reno, Nevada. They were going to rob the city of Reno for millions.

Carla thought her boyfriend, Tommy, and Tommy's older brother Gary, had things worked out. To the minute. Didn't they?

CHAPTER 1

The Dispatch Center was located in the basement of the fire station. Reno Fire Department Station 1 was a 3 story building, not including the dispatch center in the basement. The 3rd floor was where the firemen lived while on duty. The firemen on duty slept, ate, watched television, or just relaxed during their down time, between calls or "alarms." The firemen called all their calls for service "alarms." The dispatchers would call them "runs".

The second floor were the offices of all the support staff of the Reno Fire Department. From the Fire Chief, to the Assistant Fire Chief , to all the Battalion Chiefs in charge of specific areas of the Reno Fire Department, to the Fire Marshal and all the Fire Prevention staff including the investigators.

The first floor was the "apparatus floor". It was where both the fire engines of Station 1, the Rescue Squad, the ladder truck, the battalion chief's car, the boat trailer and the reserve fire engines, were parked when they were not being dispatched to a call.

When someone entered the building on the first floor, there was a long counter where a fireman, usually the new person (man or woman), would greet them and help them with directions, or fire prevention issues. The Battalion Chief's living quarters during their 24 hour shift was located about 8 feet behind the counter, in a separate room which contained a cot with appropriate bedding and a separate bathroom with shower. His door was usually closed when he was not there.

If someone entering the main door and continued walking straight, they would see to the right was the stairs. To the left of the stairs was the elevator, and down a short hall straight ahead was the door leading to the apparatus floor. The first thing you noticed when you entered thru the door was the "pole". The firemen would use the pole most of the time because the elevator was so slow, and it was the quickest route to the apparatus floor. Time was a big factor when firemen answered an alarm.

The dispatch center took up most of the basement. When getting off the elevator or stairs there was a door. A window that was approximately 4 ft from the floor was used by the dispatchers to see who was at the door before the door was opened. There was a closed circuit television camera, but it was mounted so high that usually the dispatch could only see the top of the person's head. There was a speaker to the left of the door, with a buzzer for any visitor to use, to make their presence known. On the door was a key pad that the dispatchers could use to enter the door without having to be "buzzed in". The dispatch floor was as large as a high school gymnasium. There was carpeting on the walls to cut down the noise. The flooring consisted of large square tiles that covered a sub flooring underneath. That was where all the wires and cords plugged into the radios, computers, telephones, fax machines and teletype systems, that ran the dispatch center. The dispatch center was utilized by several agencies that the Reno Police Dispatch Center dispatched for. All those agencies had contracts with the City of Reno. All the dispatchers working the graveyard shift were all "cross trained", meaning they could work any position in the dispatch center. From answering 911 calls, to dispatching Washoe County Sheriff's deputies, Reno Police officers, both of the Tribal Police agencies (Reno Sparks Tribal Police Department and the Pyramid Lake Police Department), or the Reno Fire Department.

CHAPTER 2

Carla looked at her watch again. It was 1:15 A.M. She tried to remember where everyone was. George was at the Silver Slipper. The Silver Slipper was a large casino in downtown Reno. George had said that all the rooms were occupied . No one wanted to miss Kool Klassic Nights. From the old and unusual cars, to the entertainment that was usually set up for people of all ages. Sometimes the concerts were free, and anyone could see what a good time everyone was having. The Silver Slipper always had a special permit during Kool Klassic Nights. They would close off the side street leading to the Silver Slipper. There would be live music, dancing, street vendors, and it was all open to the public with no admission charge. For George it was a security nightmare and he had tried to tell his boss, and his boss' boss that security should be tightened. They never listened to him, but they would after tonight. But, by then it would be too late. George was the security supervisor who had come up with the idea.

Charlie was at the Platinum Club. The Platinum Club was smaller than the Silver Slipper, but the Platinum Club patrons were wealthier. It was decorated to look very expensive. All the waiters and waitresses wore outfits that were dark red in color. They had to look elegant while they worked. The patrons expected more glamour and better service because they were paying more. The owners of the Platinum Club did not pay their employees much more above minimum wage. The owners believed the customers of the Platinum Club would tip the employees more than any other casino because the customers were spending more. The owners forgot that their patrons had made their money by working hard for it, or inheriting it. Not by giving it away. Not all of the Platinum Club patrons did that, but enough did to make it difficult to make ends meet. That's why Charlie signed on with George. He wasn't a security supervisor, but like George, he worked in the dispatch center there.

As soon as the casinos were aware they were being robbed, they would call Charlie, and George. But Charlie and George would not take that call or make any call to the police department. Charlie would be breaking into the safe at the Silver Slipper. It was located in the security office right next to the dispatch center. George would be doing the same at the Platinum Club.

Tommy figured between the two casinos in Reno, the bank in Lemmon Valley and the bank on Wedge Parkway, there would be several million dollars. Gary told him the Kool Klassic Nights event was the biggest money maker that Reno had.

All the people who came to Reno were looking for a good time, show off their fancy cars and spend money. The city of Reno, Nevada is only one hour's drive to Lake Tahoe. It is centrally located to other tourist areas. Truckee, Ca is located to the west of Reno. Susanville, Ca is located to the north. The capital city of Nevada is Carson City and is located just south of Reno. Reno has large casinos, large convention centers, competent bus lines through out the city and adjacent areas, and several cab companies. Tommy knew Reno is called the "biggest little city in the world".

It was probably named that because when Reno puts on an event like Kool Klassic Nights, people from all over the world come to attend. Reno looked forward to the festivities because it made millions for the city coffers. Of course the banks were keeping extra cash on hand for all the tourists.

CHAPTER 3

All of the fire stations in the City of Reno had paging alert systems, activated by the dispatch center. The pagers were used when paging out any apparatus assigned to that particular station. When the pager activated it was usually the fire engine or the truck that was assigned. Sometimes it was the rescue squad. When the station pager was activated it would set off a large loud alarm, then the dispatcher would say the equipment being sent, the type of call they were responding to, the address of the call, the district area it was assigned to and the map number. All vehicles carried maps, and if the personnel assigned to the call was unfamiliar with the address they could look it up by the map number. The district number would coincide with the fire station that was assigned that area. Because the Reno Fire Department fire stations responded to emergency, life or death situation, their paging systems were tested every day (including weekends and holidays) at 8:00 A.M. and 8:00 P.M.

Reno Fire Station Six heard the strangest page on their station pager, it was 7:10 a.m. Their usual station page to test their alert tones was done at 8:00 a.m. Luckily they were awake. Captain John James called dispatch to ask them what that last station page was. No answer. Captain James wasn't concerned. If the dispatcher was busy she wouldn't be able to answer the phone. But, if the page was important, he needed to know what kind of call they had. Captain James called the Battalion Chief on duty at Reno Fire Station One. Chief Glen Vander was just waking up, getting ready for the next Battalion Chief to relieve him. Chief Ben Torres would be arriving any minute.

When the phone rang, Chief Vander figured it must be dispatch wanting to ask a question. Instead it was Captain James from Station Six. Captain James explained about the strange station page saying, I think the dispatcher said "help me, their all dead." Captain James asked Chief Vander if the chief knew what the page was about, and if Station one had received the page too. Chief Vander said he had not received the page but would call dispatch. Captain James told Chief Vander he had tried to call dispatch but no one answered the phone. The fire battalion chief thought they were probably busy. After telling Captain James he would check into it, Chief Vander walked downstairs to the door of dispatch, that was located in the basement of Reno Fire Station One.

The dispatch center was in a secured area where the only way to enter the dispatch center was to know the combination of the door, have a key to the door, or to press the black buzzer so the dispatcher could release the door lock. Chief Vander did not have a key, nor did he know the door combination. He knew that the dispatcher monitoring the door had other duties to perform, so he waited a minute or two after pressing the buzzer. He knew they could see him on the closed circuit television so he waved at them and pointed to his badge, showing them he was a battalion chief with the Reno Fire Department. Chief Vander was a busy man and had more important things to do than stand outside the dispatch center door, waiting for someone to let him in.

After a couple of minutes, when Chief Vander did not hear the door release, nor did the dispatcher speak to him over the speaker, Chief Vander became concerned about the dispatchers. When he looked through the window of the door and saw one of the dispatchers laying on the floor, he realized that something bad, really bad, had happened in the dispatch center. He ran upstairs yelling for all the firemen to respond to the apparatus floor.

CHAPTER 4

Firemen from both shifts, the ones coming on, and the ones going off duty, were all there, standing near the battalion chief, wondering what was going on. They were listening to the battalion chief, on the phone, calling Reno Fire Station Three, asking them to send their hazmat rig to Station One for a level three hazmat assignment.

They all knew that a level three hazmat meant serious injury or death that involved a hazardous material of unknown origin. A level three calls out not only Reno Fire Department, Sparks Fire Department, the State of Nevada Hazmat Team, but also included all off duty hazmat personnel. The firemen knew this was not an exercise drill, this was the real thing. All the firemen were wondering, what happened down in dispatch?

The Battalion Chief immediately broadcasted over the P.A. system that Reno Fire Station #1 was to be evacuated immediately. The Battalion Chief ran to his office and called the Sparks Fire Department. He told them there was a level 3 hazmat at the the Reno dispatch center. Then he called Nevada Highway Patrol Dispatch and told them the same thing. The chief knew they would notify the hazmat unit for the state. Then he grabbed the car keys to the Incident Commander's Vehicle. He ordered all the firemen to move the equipment out of the station and use it to block off the streets surrounding the fire station. Truck One was used to block off all of Second Street at Evans Avenue.

Engine One was used to block off Evans Avenue north of the station. The reserve engine was used to block off Second Street east of the fire station. Truck One was moving into position to block off Second Street west of station one. While the equipment was being moved into position, Battalion Chief Vander called every fire station by phone to let them know of the hazmat situation in dispatch. Chief Vander did not want to broadcast the information on the radio because Chief Vander knew there were a lot of scanners. That, and Chief Vander knew that several of the dispatchers were married to police or fire personnel. He did not know if the dispatchers in the basement, had relatives on duty. Any of the police officers or firemen could be a relative of one or more of the dispatchers.

Officer Clark with the Reno Police Department saw the fire department had several pieces of equipment parked in the roadway blocking off all access to the fire station. Officer Clark knew something bad must have happened but he did not know what. The radio had been quiet for several hours. He did not know, but one thing was clear, Officer Clark knew if something bad had happened the dispatcher would have broadcast it on all frequencies for all the agencies. Officer Clark stopped and said,

"what's going on?" Captain Wilkinson directed Officer Clark to talk to Battalion Chief Vander. Chief Vander told officer Clark he needed to talk to the watch commander ASAP (as soon as possible).

Officer Clark radioed to dispatch asking where Sgt Lewis (the watch commander) was, but there was no response. Officer Clark knew that sometimes Sgt Lewis would need to leave the office, just to stretch his legs or get some air. Sgt. Lewis was supposed to let dispatch know where he was. But he usually never did. Sgt. Lewis expected the officers working under him to let dispatch know where they were, but the officers didn't bother either. They thought, why should they follow SOP (standard operating procedure) when their supervisor didn't. Usually the only time the officers radioed in was when they made a traffic stop, checked a business that was open to make sure everything was okay, or when they wanted dispatch to know where they were. When Sgt. Lewis received the radio call from Officer Clark, his first instinct was to ignore it. After all, he had worked twelve hours and he was tired. He was ready to go home. Sgt. Lewis used his cell phone to call and asked Officer Clark if he could call the Battalion Chief by phone, when he reached the police station. The battalion chief told Officer Clark he needed to see Sgt. Lewis in person. Sgt. Lewis agreed to stop at Fire Station One on his way back to the police station. Sgt. Lewis decided he only had thirty minutes more of his shift. He thought to himself, it couldn't be that bad!

What ever it was, he would just pass it on to day shift and go home. When Chief Vander told Sgt. Lewis he needed to talk to him in person, that the information was critical but needed to be relayed to him in person, Sgt. Lewis felt apprehensive about it. Sgt. Lewis had worked a long shift like all the other officers. Sgt. Lewis had a sneaking suspicion that he was not going to be off duty for a long time.

CHAPTER 5

Rob Matthews was the Detective Sergeant who was assigned to investigate major crimes that occurred in the city of Reno. His wife Caryn, was working graveyard shift. She was working mandatory overtime during Kool Klassic Nights. She got off work at 7:00 a.m. Rob knew the mandatory overtime had Caryn working a fourteen hour day. Rob looked at his watch and saw it was a little after 8:00 a.m. Rob wondered where Caryn was. She probably had to stop at the store and get some groceries before she came home. Either that, or she was going to bring something home for breakfast, to surprise Rob. Today was Rob's day off and maybe they would spend it together in bed. Rob loved Caryn very much and every day that love just grew stronger.

Rob was just getting out of the shower when he heard his pager beeping. He thought to himself, "don't they know I'm off today? This better be an emergency!" He looked at the print out on his pager and had to look twice. The police chief's home phone number was listed on the pager. Rob had never been paged by the Chief before. Something big was happening in the city. Why didn't dispatch, especially Caryn, call him and let him know?

When he called, the chief said, "My office! Ten minutes! Rob it's bad! It looks like everyone in the dispatch center is dead or dying! All we know is that the Fire Department Battalion Chief can see one dispatcher down through the window of the dispatch door! There is no response from inside the center! They have a hazmat situation! We're handling this as a terrorist act! "You know I have the utmost respect and I care about all the men and women that work for me, but thank goodness Caryn is off work today!"

Rob felt like he had just been punched in the stomach. Rob closed his eyes, took a deep breath and said very slowly, "Caryn's at work, she was working mandatory overtime."

Rob felt numb. He could not believe what the Chief had just said. Rob now knew why Caryn had not come home. Rob was not going to spend all day making love to his wife. Rob may not have a wife .

CHAPTER 6

Rob Matthews and Caryn had been married for five years. They had worked together for nine years. They had worked together for almost four years without ever meeting. Rob was hired by the City of Reno Police Department twelve years ago. Rob and Caryn had both worked for the Reno Police Department for several years before they met, fell in love, and got married.

When Rob was hired by the Reno Police Department he was married to Sally, his first wife. They both moved to Reno from Las Vegas.

He as a police officer and Sally as a dispatcher. They were hired at the same time. Sally became a dispatch supervisor three years later. It was at about the same time that Rob made detective.

Maybe the added stress of Sally's promotion was what caused the collapse of their marriage. Sally said she had more responsibilities now. At first Rob was very proud of Sally and how much pride she took in her new promotion. Then Rob started feeling neglected. On their only day off together, out of the week, they usually spent their day catching up on their lovemaking. Or discuss what had happened during their work week, their goals and their future vacation plans. But Sally started saying she had a headache from the stress of the job and did not feel like making love or talking.

All she did was stay in bed and rest, watch television or read. She ignored Rob. She locked Rob out of her life. When Rob asked Sally to demote back to a dispatcher, thinking Sally would be happy with the move, Sally refused saying she was just getting acclimated and would get used to the stress. She would be better soon. Rob suspected that there was something more going on than just the added stress of her job.

Rob came to the conclusion that Sally was having an affair.

Caryn was working on Sally's shift and Sally would talk about Caryn and what a good dispatcher she was. By what Sally said, Rob got the impression that Sally was jealous of Caryn. One day on Rob's day off, Rob decided to surprise Sally at work. He brought lunch to Sally so they could share lunch. Sally's favorite lunch was broccoli and beef from the chinese restaurant in Bill's Casino. When he arrived he stood by the entrance to the dispatch floor, trying to see if he recognized anyone. Sally always complained about the turnover in dispatch. Sally said she had more new dispatchers working on her shift than any other shift. Rob wasn't sure if she was boasting or complaining. Rob remembered Sally saying that the fire department dispatcher is the least busy dispatcher unless she has a working fire. When he could not see Sally on the dispatch floor. He walked over to the fire dispatcher. She had just dispatched one of the fire engines to a heart attack at Bill's Casino. He noticed she was very competent juggling the fire radio and the 9-1-1 lines. That's when he saw the cell phone. The on duty dispatcher supervisor, Sally, was to have the dispatch supervisor's cell phone while she was at work. Caryn had it, which meant Sally had left work. But where did she go, and with whom?

The fire dispatcher realized someone was watching her and looked up. When Rob saw the dispatcher's face he wondered what a beautiful woman, like this one, was doing working dispatch in the basement of the fire station. Sally had never told him that dispatch had hired a beauty queen working here.

Then Rob saw her name tag on her uniform. It read Caryn Stevens, so this was Caryn. Caryn wondered what this good looking guy was doing in dispatch carrying bags of Chinese food. Caryn identified herself as the acting supervisor and asked if she could help him. He asked Caryn, "where is Sally?" Caryn explained that Sally always had lunch with Lieutenant Mills, who was in charge of dispatch. Caryn said, [3]they had lunch every day and would probably be gone for another hour. Now Rob understood why Sally was ignoring him. She was screwing her boss.

Not wanting to look like a fool, and after losing his appetite, Rob told her he had brought lunch for the dispatchers because he enjoyed working with them. He told Caryn that the dispatchers did not get the recognition they deserved.

Rob appreciated the job the dispatchers do, knowing they were an essential part of any police or fire department, but the least mentioned when it came time to give words of appreciation from the public.

He knew that everyone in the police department was notorious gossips. He asked Caryn, "where does Sally and the Lieutenant go to lunch?" Rob was surprised when Caryn answered that she did not know where they went, but she would take a message to give Sally. Rob told her he would talk to Sally later, and he left.

Rob decided that he would rather give the food away, than look like an idiot. After all Sally was his wife. Shouldn't he know if she has lunch with her boss, every day? Rob knew there was more involved than lunch and decided to confront Sally when she got home. Sally and Rob worked different shifts which meant Rob did not get to have that talk he wanted

After several weeks of wondering what was going on between Lieutenant Mills and Sally, Sally came to Rob and asked him for a divorce. She said she had found someone else. She said she fell out of love with Rob and in love with Lieutenant Mark Mills. Rob did not tell Sally he suspected something had been going on. Rob thought he would be devastated about the breakup with Sally, but all he felt was relief. Maybe he had fallen out of love with Sally too.

CHAPTER 7

Rob could not forget Caryn. Sometimes he would call her, just to say "hi." Rob found out she was not only beautiful on the outside but she was a beautiful person on the inside. Rob was surprised that Caryn was shy. She was hesitant to date Rob, because of Sally. But she was just as attracted to him as he was to her.

After Rob and Sally divorced, Rob started dating Caryn and as they say, the rest was history.

Sally had a long lunch with Mark Mills every day. Usually they picked up lunch from a fast food place and went to a motel where they ate lunch in bed. It would be the same bed they had just made love in. Sally thought their love making was their little secret but most of the patrol officers knew the lieutenant's personal car and saw it was parked at a different motel each day. Officers were notorious gossips.

Reno had lots of motels and they went to a different motel for almost three weeks straight before they ran out and started the cycle over again. Both of them thought they were so smart keeping their affair a secret.

Sally had expected Mark Mills to divorce his wife, but surprisingly it didn't happen. Mark told Sally he loved his wife not her. Sally, being the woman scorned, made sure she was the injured party involved. Her allegation of sexual harassment and sexual misconduct went to an internal affairs investigation. Mark Mills was found not guilty of sexual harassment but was found guilty of sexual misconduct. He was suspended for two weeks without pay, demoted to sergeant and transferred from dispatch to patrol. As far as Sally knew he was currently working graveyard shift.

Surprisingly, Mark's wife forgave him. It probably helped that he cried like a baby, told her he had never cheated on her before, and never would again.

CHAPTER 8

Rob was promoted to being a detective in Major Crimes, and shortly after that promoted to sergeant. He was assigned to handle all major crimes involving terrorist acts that occurred in the City of Reno. He and Caryn were married six years ago, after dating for two years. He loved her deeply and appreciated every minute he spent with her. Working different shifts was difficult but they embraced any time they spent together. After two years, they decided to start a family. So far Caryn had miscarried once and was afraid to try again. Rob was anxious to start a family, but today, Rob was so afraid for Caryn. He was frightened to think they may never have any more time together. Caryn could be dead in the dispatch center.

Rob was sure he would feel different if Caryn was no longer in his life. Right now, besides the worry for Caryn, all Rob felt was anger for who ever had hurt his wife. And he felt a duty to do his job and find the asshole who attacked his wife and her fellow workers and friends.

Rob would not jump to conclusions. He had to believe they would be okay. He hurriedly dressed and ran out to his car. When he turned on the car, he did not hear the usual radio traffic. He reached for the radio microphone to call dispatch and let them know he was en-route to dispatch. Every time he got in his assigned detective unit, he would say "Reno, Ida 630." This time there was no response. Rob had never known a time when there was not a voice on the other end of the radio saying "go ahead Ida 630". Rob felt a cold chill and wondered if the dispatchers, especially Caryn was all right. Rob was not very religious but he said a quick prayer asking God to keep Caryn safe.

He wondered how long it would take before they knew anything on their condition.

CHAPTER 9

R ob knew that the Sergeant or the Lieutenant of patrol would contact the deputy chief in charge of communications as SOP (standard operating procedure). The chain of command would continue down from the Deputy Chief to the Lieutenant, the Lieutenant to the administrative supervisor, to one of the many dispatch supervisors. Rob knew that like the great flood of 1997, when dispatch was evacuated, the emergency dispatch center at Ninth Street and Wells Avenue was utilized. Right now there was no dispatch center for Reno Police, Washoe County Sheriffs, Reno fire department, University of Reno Police, Reno Sparks Tribal Police or Pyramid Lake Tribal police. Rob knew that the other agencies could patch with another radio frequency, for example if Reno Police

Department asked assistance from Washoe County Sheriff's Departent, the radio dispatcher could patch the two radios together, so the Reno Police dispatcher would handle all the units on the call. The dispatcher would close the channel so the units not assigned to the call could switch to another frequency. But the dispatchers for those agencies were unavailable to patch. There were no dispatchers to do anything.

There was no one to answer the 911 emergency lines. The citizens that lived in the greater Reno jurisdictions would call 911 to help them with their problems. There was no one to answer the phone call about a barking dog complaint, all the way to the hurried phone about a heart attack, or the hysterical calls of a baby choking. The Reno Police Dispatch Center answered all the 911 lines for Northern Nevada. Rob wondered about the 911 calls. Rob knew that if the Reno Dispatch Center did not answer them, they went unanswered . Rob had heard that if a major accident or major incident occurred in northern Nevada, the dispatch center would receive so many calls, they averaged twenty 911 calls a minute, just in the Reno Dispatch Center alone. Rob knew there were usually three dispatchers, or four if they were lucky, to answer all the phones, including the 911 lines. It boggled Rob's mind to picture them juggling calls while trying to remain calm and keep the caller calm. Rob knew that a police dispatcher's job was the most stressful job there was. Rob would joke with Caryn and tell "you couldn't pay me enough dispatch.

CHAPTER 10

Rob remembered stopping to bring lunch to Caryn about six months ago. Caryn had given him the code for the door since he was member of the police department and was the husband to one of the dispatchers. Luckily, that day he did not have to wait for a dispatcher to open the door. When he walked in he could her phones ringing and a very loud alarm that screeched every minute. Rob remembered hearing Caryn complaining about the "stinger". Now he knew why. He was getting a headache just listening to it for the past three minutes since he had arrived. Sometimes he could not understand why Caryn loved the work she did. Like now. Rob found Caryn dispatching for the Reno Police Department green frequency which meant she was working the main police radio frequency. Rob had heard some of the officers complain that the radio frequency was so busy, they should have two radio frequencies for Reno Police. Luckily, today they had two frequencies opened. Caryn was the dispatcher for the north and central police units and the dispatcher for the University of Nevada Reno Police officers. The police units working the city south of the Truckee River were working on yellow frequency.

When Rob brought the food (a hamburger, fries and a strawberry shake), she smiled at him, blew him a kiss and kept acknowledging or dispatching to the 35 units she was responsible for. Rob kissed her on the back of her head and walked out. He did not want to distract her. Caryn had told Rob before, that she would fall into a rhythm that worked for her. He could see that she was there. He just hoped she could eat her lunch while it was still hot, but he doubted it.

CHAPTER 11

The non emergency lines would probably also continue ringing with no one to answer. Rob knew from what Caryn had told him that people called for some pretty silly reasons. One man called on 911 and said his watch stopped and he needed the time.

When Caryn told him that 911 was for emergencies only, he told her it was an emergency because he had an appointment and needed to know that time so he would not be late. When she told him the time, and it turned out he was already late, he cussed her out and hung up on her. Another call was a little old lady who wanted an officer to check out her house because the aliens had invaded her space and were camped out in her attic. She told Caryn they came down at night and took the cookies from her refrigerator. Caryn sent an officer, who took the time to have a cup of tea with the lonely sweet old lady. Officer Alrich would stop by and check periodically on Mrs. Moore after that call. If he could not make it, he asked the volunteer SAVE unit to do it. The SAVE units were a group of seniors, old enough to be retired but young enough to enjoy themselves, who volunteered to assist the officers by making special appearances at local schools, doing extra patrols and contacting people like Mrs. Moore who got lonely and did not have any family. It was difficult for Mrs. Moore to walk, and she could not get out very often.

Rob stopped worrying about how the city was going to reprogram the 911 lines. He wondered if they would to go to the emergency dispatch center or to the Sparks Dispatch Center. Rob knew the two departments helped each other out, but he did not know if it was even possible if the phone lines could be rerouted. Sparks could patch their radios with Reno Police or Washoe County but they would not patch with both, fearing the added work load would make it next to impossible for their dispatchers to handle.

Rob knew that during emergencies, like the great flood of 1997, dispatch was evacuated to the emergency center at Ninth Street and Wells Avenue. The Deputy Chief in charge of communications would decide when they could get the emergency dispatch center together. He would have to contact the Lieutenant in charge of communications so he could contact any off duty supervisors. It would be at least a couple of hours before they had the emergency dispatch center manned with enough dispatchers to handle all the radio frequencies needed, not to mention enough people to answer phones. Or even if the phones were connected.

Rob knew that not all 9-1-1 calls were life or death emergencies. Rob remembered the 9-11 call Caryn took while he stopped by dispatch to visit. The man was very rude on the phone. He called 9-1-1 because his neighbors children were playing basketball. The man told Caryn that she better send officers over right away, to tell the kids to watch television or play video games, so they wouldn't make any more noise. When Caryn tried to get information from him, the man yelled so loud at Caryn, Rob could hear the guy four feet away from the phone. Rob wanted to take the phone away from Caryn and tell the damned idiot that kids make noise, let them be kids! But Caryn handled it. She was able to calm him down to a point where he stopped yelling. Rob felt sorry for the neighbor, and the kids.

CHAPTER 12

Rob remembered when he realized how talented Caryn was, and not just as a dispatcher. Caryn told Rob, when they were still dating, that she would get a feeling about the phone calls she answered. Or the radio calls that she dispatched. Caryn dispatched Rob to a suspicious circumstances call. Rob was a detective. Rob knew that detectives were not sent on an initial call until an officer and a sergeant had time to arrive at the scene. Rob knew that protocol had to be followed. After the sergeant spoke to the officers on scene, the sergeant evaluated the situation, then asked for a detective, if it was necessary to do more followup. Then the detective would respond, leaving the officer free to respond to the next call.

Rob was getting ready to call dispatch by phone, and ask Caryn why she was sending him, when his cell phone rang. When he saw the caller id, and saw it was dispatch, he smiled. Nine times out of ten, when Rob thought about calling Caryn, she would call him first.

Caryn said to Rob, ""Rob, the mother at this house just called to report her eleven year old son as a runaway. She said she last saw him last night when he went to bed." Caryn said "Rob, I have a bad feeling about this one. I think the boy is dead." Rob felt cold chills. Caryn never gave Rob information about a case unless Rob asked for it. Rob knew Caryn got "feelings" about most of her calls, but almost never acted on them, because the Reno Police Officers and the Washoe County Deputies were very good at their jobs. They usually got the correct story right away. Besides, Caryn did not want anyone to think she was crazy. Sometimes Caryn "suggested" what to look for, if she felt it was necessary.

Rob asked Caryn if she had sent an officer yet. Caryn said since the call had come in as a priority three, the beat officer would look at his M.D.T.(mobile dispatch terminal) and dispatch himself, when he was available. Rob knew Caryn did not like to bring attention to herself, especially when Caryn was neversure if her feelings were correct, or not. Rob asked Caryn to let the area Watch Commander, Sgt. Cruz, know that she had talked to him about the call pending. Rob was going to go to the house and talk to the mother. He would take a look around the boy's room. Rob knew and respected Sgt. Cruz. In fact, it hadn't been too long ago that Rob and Ron Cruz were in the police break room at the same time. Ron mentioned how he enjoyed working with Caryn. How professional Caryn was. She was his favorite dispatcher. Ron told Rob that Caryn always seemed to know if a call would go "sideways." That was a polite way of saying it was going to be a "cluster fuck", or "go to shit in a big way."

When Rob got there, he sat in the car for a couple of minutes, looking at the house and the neighbors houses. If something happened inside the house, the neighbors would have heard, since the houses were practically on top of each other. Rob knew this was a low income neighborhood. Most of the houses had a rundown look to them. Almost all of them had paint fading in patches, showing neglect. Rob was just getting out of the car when Ron Cruz pulled up. Rob walked back to the patrol car. Ron got out of the car and was just putting his sergeant's hat on, when Rob approached the driver's door. Ron was one of those sergeants who not only followed orders, but made sure the men and women who worked with him did too. Ron sounded mad. He told Rob "Caryn called me on my cell phone. She said she asked you to come to this call. She told me she felt that the mom was lying and the boy was in danger. After reading the call, I called the mom. She doesn't sound upset. In fact, she sounded resigned to the fact that her son is a runaway. She told me her son ran away once before, but never over night." Ron told Rob "I don't think there is a problem here, but I wanted to tell you in person. I think Caryn has gone too far this time." Rob said to Ron "I do not have anything pressing, and since I was in the area I decided to check if the boy is at risk." Rob understood what Ron was saying, but Ron did not know how accurate Caryn's predictions were. Rob felt the least he could do was check it out. Caryn knew she could get into big trouble by not following SOP, and chain of command. If she thought it was that important, at least he could take a look around. Rob told Ron "since I'm already here, I might as well go talk to the mother." When Rob walked to the front door of the house, he noticed the walk way was littered with leaves, the same as the yard. The grass hadn't been mowed recently. Compared to the other houses, the yard looked like it hadn't been mowed for quite some time. In fact the weeds bordering the walk was so high, it was hard to see the front door from the street. By the time Rob got to the door, there was a very large female adult standing at the open door. She was probably 5'4" tall, but she looked like a mack truck, since she was about 5'4" wide. She appeared to be clean and sober (something Rob was watching for). Rob introduced himself as a detective with the Reno Police Department. She looked at Rob and said "the last time I reported Tom missing, they sent a policeofficer, not a detective." Rob explained he happened to be in the area, and decided to stop and see if Tom was a runaway or missing under suspicious circumstances.

Mrs. Lawson, the mother, told Rob that her son and herself had been involved in an argument the night before. Diane Lawson told Rob that Tom wanted to go swimming in the Truckee River while she was at work. She told him no. Tom had not done his chores, including mowing the front lawn. Tom yelled at her, saying she wouldn't know if he went swimming since she would be at work anyways. Diane told Rob that she worked at the local Denny's as one of their managers. She was concerned he would make good on his threat. Diane was able to leave work two hours earlier than usual. When she got home, Tom wasn't there. She called Tom's friends who had not seen him. She checked with her neighbors. One of the neighbors told Diane she had seen him leaving the house at about 10 A.M. carrying a small inner tube and a beach towel. The Truckee River was approximately 1 and ½ miles away from the house. Diane told Rob she drove from home, to the river, but did not see Tom. Rob asked to see Tom's room. The room was an average sized room with a twin bed and lots of "Pokemon" posters on the walls. When Rob asked Diane about the posters, since the posters seemed to be more for the younger children, Diane explained that Tom was a little slow for his age, and acted like a nine year old, not an eleven year old, soon to be twelve years old. She said Tom was bipolar and taking medication. Diane was not sure if Tom had taken his medication before he left the house. Rob now knew why Caryn had been so concerned. None of that information had been in the call. Rob used his cell phone to call Ron Cruz and relay the information. Now Tom was considered a priority missing child, at risk, instead of a low priority runaway. Ron told Rob that he would be on his way to the residence. Sgt. Cruz then advised Caryn via police radio, that the priority of the runaway juvenile was to be changed to a priority one, top priority. Sgt. Cruz then asked for all available officers to respond to begin a search for Tom. They had a mentally challenged minor who was possibly swimming by himself in the Truckee River. Rob knew that the heavy snow over the past winter months had made the Truckee River dangerous for anyone who was not a strong swimmer. It was definitely not safe for an eleven year old boy who was there with no one to save him, if he needed to be saved.

Rob called his sergeant and told him he would be tied up on a missing child call. Rob gave him all the particulars except for one. Caryn told Rob that she thought the boy was dead. Did that mean he had drowned? The only way for Rob to find out was to ask Caryn.

CHAPTER 13

R ob called Caryn's supervisor, Roxanne Newton. Rob liked Roxie. Roxie didn't use her position as supervisor to intimidate the dispatchers. Rob knew that some dispatch supervisors played favorites. Sometimes a supervisor placed on or more of the dispatchers on phones for more that half of their shift, because it gave their favorite dispatchers more radio time. The favored dispatcher would reciprocate by buying lunch for the supervisor, or making a coffee run to the closest Starbucks. The favored dispatcher, if assigned phones, was usually found sitting with the supervisor on the "bridge."

The dispatch floor was about the size of a small gymnasium. It had "consoles scattered around the room. On the north wall was the radio dispatchers for the police agencies. On the west wall was the phone bank. There were enough phone positions for five dispatchers to answer all incoming non emergency lines and 911. On the south wall, directly opposite of the police radio positions was the "bridge." And on the east wall was the "fire pod". The fire dispatcher, and the fire back up dispatcher always sat in the "fire pod."

The "bridge" was a raised platform that the supervisor on duty always sat at. It had all the radio frequencies, in case the supervisor had to take over for any reason. It contained all incoming phone lines, so the supervisor made sure all in coming calls were answered in a timely manner. It also had the computer, for the supervisor to monitor all the calls that were pending, or had been dispatched.

Rob called Roxie and asked her what time Caryn had her lunch break. Roxie looked at the dispatch schedule and saw that Caryn was scheduled for a lunch break at 1600 hrs (4 P.M.). Rob looked at his watch and saw it was 1530 hrs. Rob said he would stop by then to visit Caryn while she ate lunch. Rob then called Caryn. Caryn answered the phone which was at one of the police radio positions. Caryn asked Rob if he could hold on while she acknowledged the units on the radio. Two minutes later Caryn got back om the phone. Rob told her was going to meet her for lunch. Caryn told Rob she was hungry for a hot pastrami sandwich from her favorite sandwich shop "Bojos". Rob laughed and said "of course." Rob hung up and thought "I've created a monster". Rob had taken Caryn to Bojos almost every time they went out on a date. Bojos was both their favorite place for hot pastrami sandwiches. There were other items on the menu but neither Rob nor Caryn ever ordered anything else. The hot pastrami sandwiches were that good.

CHAPTER 14

Rob made it to dispatch with five minutes to spare. He met Caryn in the dispatch lunch room. The lunch room was located just off the dispatch floor. It contained a large rectangular table with about 8 chairs around it. It also contained a stove and a refrigerator, and a microwave. Dispatchers had 30 minutes for lunch. Usually, that meant bringing something in that could be "nuked" in the microwave, and enough time to eat it. Or, going to a fast drive thru place, and coming back and having enough time to "scarf it down" before returning to the dispatch floor. Or, driving to a slow drive thru, or running inside to order and pick up your food, then being able to make it back on time, to return to the dispatch floor, then eating the food while talking on the radio and/or the phone. If that occurred, usually by the time you ate lunch it was cold and unappetizing. Rob tried to get away as often as he could, to meet Caryn for lunch, but it didn't always happen. It worked out today.

While eating their sandwiches Caryn asked Rob about the missing boy. Rob told her what the mother had told him. Caryn said "he was on his way to the river, but he never made it." Then to Rob's surprise Caryn started to cry. She kept saying "he didn't want to go." Then Caryn cried harder. Roxie came rushing out to the lunch room, after hearing Caryn crying. Rob told Roxie that Caryn wasn't feeling well and asked if he could take her home. Roxie asked Caryn if that was what she wanted. Even though Rob was a detective, he was still a man. Roxie wanted to make sure Caryn and Rob had not been involved in a family dispute. Caryn was still crying, but at least it wasn't the loud sobbing from earlier. Caryn nodded her head yes. Roxie told Rob to wait while she got Caryn's purse and her headset. Roxie also wanted to let the other dispatchers know that Caryn was leaving because she was ill. Rob carefully helped Caryn to her feet and was walking slowly to the door when Roxie brought Caryn's belongings to her. Roxie gave Caryn a hug and told her she hoped Caryn felt better. Caryn knew she would not feel better until she told Rob what she knew. She would not feel better until they found Tom, dead or alive.

Rob carefully helped Caryn into his car. He pulled out his cell phone and called his sergeant. He asked

Sgt. Jacobs to meet him at Rob and Caryn's home. Rob knew this was too much for him to do by himself. He trusted Sgt. Jacobs and knew Jack

Jacobs would know what to do. Sgt. Jacobs told Rob his ETA (estimated time of arrival) was fifteen minutes. Rob thought, that was perfect. Rob and Caryn would be home in seven minutes. Enough time for Rob to help Caryn calm down. Also enough time for Rob to decide how to explain to Jack what Caryn knew and how she knew it.

CHAPTER 15

When Jack arrived, Caryn was no longer crying. But, she looked so sad it frightened Rob, not only for Caryn's sake but for Tom too. Rob explained to Jack that he had received unsolicited and unconventional help when he cleared most of the cases assigned to him. The person who had helped him did not want to be recognized, because it was a little unorthodox. Several large police departments around the country used psychics. But, Reno Police Department was not one of the them. Luckily, Jack had an open mind and knew that some cases were not possible to solve without assistance from people who saw more than most of us did.

What surprised Jack was that Rob told him his help came from Caryn. Jack had overheard some of the police officers talk about calls they had been dispatched to. The officers sometimes thought Caryn was crazy to send a cover unit to a "one unit" call. But nine times out of ten it ended up that the officer needed the cover unit that had been sent. Word spread throughout the patrol officers that if Caryn had anything to do with the call, entering the information from a phone call, or dispatch the call, if she sent you a cover unit, you accepted it with no questions asked. Now Jack understood why Rob was so concerned.

Rob told Jack about how he got involved in the missing child case. Rob told Jack he was afraid it was a lot more than the information they had. A lot more. Rob was afraid that Tom had been kidnapped, and possibly murdered.

Jack was shocked. There was no indication of that from the evidence they found at the residence. There was no forced entry. Nothing missing except a beach towel, Tom's swimming trunks and a small inner tube. Jack thought "did Rob have an eye witness?

Rob told Jack what Caryn had said in the dispatch lunch room. "He was on his way to the river, but he didn't make it." Rob told Jack he was sure there was more but Caryn had become hysterical. Rob said he had never seen her so upset.

Jack nodded his head, then turned and looked at Caryn. Caryn appeared to be seeing something they couldn't see. Suddenly Caryn jumped up and yelled "Rob, he's still alive. Thank God he's still alive." Rob rushed to Caryn's side. Rob wanted to hug her but was afraid she would lose the vision she had of Tom. Rob gave Jack a look as if to say "let me talk to her, I know what to do." Jack nodded his head, took out his notebook and a small pocket recorder. He turned on the recorder, not wanting to miss anything. The notebook was used for quick notes he could pass on to Sgt. Cruz who was in charge of the search for the child.

Caryn, with tears in her eyes, told Rob that Tom had been taken by a man driving a van. He had stopped and asked Tom where the best place was to put a raft in the Truckee River. The man told Tom he had an experimental raft that could go faster than anything, including Tom's inner tube, could go. The man asked Tom if he wanted to be the copilot. When Tom said "oh yeah", the man told Tom to hop in the van. Tom did not know the man, but he seemed nice. His mom always told Tom to stay away from bad strangers but Tom knew this man wasn't a bad stranger since he was so nice.

The man drove away and headed the opposite direction from the Truckee River. He explained to Tom that he forgot to bring his lunch. He asked Tom what his favorite sandwich was. Tom said "I like tuna sandwiches with pickles." The man chuckled and said he did too. That was what he had made for lunch. He told Tom he would make another sandwich for Tom.

When they got to the house, Tom was given a glass of kool-aid to drink. Tom thought it had a funny taste, but then Tom thought, that's because it wasn't the kind his mom always gave him. He liked the fruit punch flavor, and this tasted like it was maybe the cherry flavor. Tom fell asleep eating his sandwich.

CHAPTER 16

Caryn told Rob she thought Tom had died because he just slipped to the floor and never moved. Caryn told Rob she just saw Tom open his eyes for a moment, but it looked like he fell asleep again. Rob asked Caryn where the suspect was. Caryn said she did not know. She could only see Tom. She had not seen him since Tom woke up, but she could identify him, since she saw him when he picked up Tom.

Rob knew time was of the essence. They had to find Tom before something worse happened to him. Had he been abducted by a child molester? Or, a child murderer? Or, someone who wanted a "son" so bad that he had taken Tom to take care of him.

Caryn told Rob she could show them the area where the suspect drove to. She had seen a glimpse of the house that the suspect had taken Tom to. She knew the van was a light blue van, and had a "porthole" type window on the passenger's side. She was pretty sure she could identify it if she saw it again. Jack decided to believe what Caryn told him.

Jack and Rob decided to keep Caryn's name out of the investigation as much as possible.

Caryn told Rob to drive to Tom's house first. When they got in the area and was within a block of Tom's house, Caryn said "now drive straight ahead until you get to 4th st. From 4th Street, go towards Sierra St. Tom walked to Sierra Street and walking southbound when the van stopped and picked him up.

Rob thought that a lot of people must have seen one little boy get into a light blue van. But no one had called in to the tip line yet. A lot of people had seen various little boys matching Tom's description, but none of them had been Tom. All leads were being followed up on as quickly as possible. Jack and Rob were afraid that Tom was running out of time.

CHAPTER 17

Caryn said "at the next corner turn right." Rob turned right on 3rd Street. They continued for several blocks until Caryn told Rob to turn right again. Rob turned onto Ralston St. Caryn told Rob it wasn't much further. In the 600 block of Ralston Street, Caryn yelled "that's it. It's right behind that yellow house." The house she was pointing to was a small one story house that was behind the larger two story yellow house. The smaller house looked like it may have been a guest house, but was now used as a rental house. The house was an ugly faded darkgreen house. There was a small one car garage right next to it. The long driveway went past the yellow house. It looked like both houses sat on one acre of land. It was a large lot and in an older part of Reno.

Rob did not see a vehicle, much less the blue van. It was possible it was in the garage and out of sight, since the garage door was down. Caryn told Rob she never saw the man use the garage when he arrived with Tom. But, then again, Caryn only saw

Tom in her vision after he was abducted. She did not see the suspect after he arrived at the house.

Rob and Jack drove and parked two houses beyond the suspect's residence. They parked on the opposite side of the street. They got out of the vehicle and told Caryn to stay in the car. They walked up to the door of the house they parked in front of. When they knocked on the door, a nice looking woman answered the door. She was about 50 years old. She had that exasperated look that looked like she expected Rob and Jack to be salesmen. They identified themselves as Reno Police Detectives, and asked the lady if she knew who lived in the house behind 683 Ralston Street. She told them "I don't know which house that is." When Rob pointed out that it was the dark green house behind the yellow two story house, she pursed her lips and said "Oh, that one. He moved out a month ago. And good riddance. He was always drunk, or drinking and becoming drunk. And he was always a mean drunk." She said "he had a woman and a small boy living with him but they left him about three months ago. He wouldn't let the boy play outside. One time the woman was outside and I called to her. I said hello and waved. She waved back and started to walk over here when that bastard of a boyfriend or husband came out and yelled at her to get her ass inside the house." The woman continued, "a couple of weeks later I saw her, and her son leaving the house. They left in a cab. I never saw them again." Then she said, "that same day I had to call the police because the man was in his front yard. He was as drunk as a skunk, yelling obscenities. When the officers arrived they told the man to go inside and sleep it off. He moved out less than a week later."

Rob asked the woman what kind of car the man drove. She said he drove a baby blue colored van. She told Rob and Jack that she did not know what the man's name was. She said she doubted he had ever talked to any of the neighbors. When Rob asked when she last saw the man, or the van, she told Rob she last saw him about a month ago when he moved out. She told them she had never seen the man talk to any of the neighbors. She never saw any visitors at the house. Jack thanked her for her time, and she closed the door.

CHAPTER 18

Jack and Rob then walked over to the garage, next to the house, and looked in the window. There was no van, or any other vehicle inside. They were deciding what to do when Caryn got out of the car and walked over to Rob. She said very calmly "the boy is inside this house. He is in a bedroom that faces the back of the house, off the kitchen. He is asleep on the floor. I think he was drugged." Then Caryn started to cry softly and said "Rob, he is having difficulty breathing." She said "Rob, he doesn't have much time."

Rob looked to Jack as if to say "what do you want me to do now." Jack was married and had two young boys, four and six years old. They and his wife were his world. He loved his family very much. If it was one of his son's inside the house, he wouldn't question the decision. He decided not to question it now. He would break into the house anyway he could, to save his son. It was only right to break in to save this child. He would not be able to live with himself if he had been able to save the boy, and did not at least try.

Jack ran to the back door and tried to turn the door knob. It was locked. Jack used his foot to kick the door. Then he used his shoulder to force the door open. The door banged against the wall. Jack and Rob, both with guns drawn, slowly entered the house.

They could not hear anything. They noticed there was no furniture they could see. While Rob checked the rest of the small house, Jack went to the bedroom that was located next to the kitchen. It was exactly like Caryn described it. Except for one thing. The bedroom was empty.

Rob came in shortly after Jack. Then Caryn ran into the room. Without stopping she ran to the door of the closet. The door to the closet had been hidden behind the bedroom door. Before Rob or Jack could stop her, she opened the closet door and there was Tom, laying on the floor of the closet. He was not breathing.

Rob handed her his handy talky and told her to call dispatch to ask for an ambulance. Caryn keyed the mike and said "1630 Reno." When the dispatcher told Caryn to go ahead, Caryn said "1630, we need an ambulance, the fire department, FIS (Field Investigation Services), and Sgt Cruz to respond to 683 Ralston St. The house to the rear. We have located the missing child. Advise the ambulance and the fire department that it is a cardiac arrest. The child is not breathing. CPR is in progress." The dispatcher acknowledged and immediately called for N230 to respond to 638 Ralston Street, to meet with 1630 on scene.

By the time the Reno Fire Department arrived and took over CPR, the ambulance pulled up. When

Sgt. Cruz arrived, the firemen and the ambulance crew had stabilized the boy, and were placing him into the ambulance on a stretcher.

CHAPTER 19

Caryn just stood there for the longest time. Caryn was so relieved they had found Tom. She hoped physically, Tom was going to be okay. Mentally was different matter. While Ron, Jack and Rob were talking, Caryn looked around the room. She saw an old blanket that looked like it had been hand made. It was very dirty and it was hard to tell what color it really was. For some reason, Caryn was drawn to the blanket, and she knew that if she touched it, she may get a vision of the suspect and where he may be at. Caryn was just reaching for it when one of the FIS technicians yelled at her and told her it was part of the crime scene. Since it was part of the crime scene it was not to be touched by anyone. Rob overheard what the technician said, and how he said it. Rob was pissed. Rob knew that if it hadn't been for Caryn they would never have found Tom on time. If Caryn thought the blanket was important then Rob was going to get it for her. Rob went to Caryn's side, took her hand and asked her what she was going to do. She told Rob that she had a very strong urge to touch the blanket. Rob walked over to Jack and took him aside. When Rob explained the situation, Jack talked to the FIS technician. He told the technician, Sam Powell, he wanted the blanket. He told Sam that the blanket was not part of the evidence, but a crucial part of the investigation. Jack knew that Sam had a reputation for being an asshole at crime scenes. But Jack also knew he was very good at his job. Jack told Sam he appreciated Sam being professional, but Jack needed to take the blanket. Jack told Sam he could contact his supervisor, but Jack would then have to tell how Sam was hindering Jack's investigation. Sam said "fine, take it. But will I get it back?" Jack said he would let him know when he no longer needed it.

Jack very carefully placed the small blanket into an evidence bag. Jack planned on returning the blanket to Sam. Jack hoped there was no evidence lost while it was in Caryn's possession. Then Jack, Caryn, Rob and Ron walked back to their cars. When they got back to the cars, Ron got into Jack's vehicl, and sat in the front passenger seat. Caryn and Rob sat in the back seat. Jack turned around and told Caryn that Ron was now privy to all the information, including how they were able to locate Tom so quickly.

CHAPTER 20

Caryn closed her eyes and put her head back. Caryn never wanted anyone to know what she could do. All her life, while growing up, she knew things she should never have known. When she tried to tell her mom about some of the things, her mom looked at her like she was crazy. Her dad was never home. He was always working. And when he wasn't working, he was always visiting someone, or helping the neighbors. Caryn remembered the neighbors seemed to need help a lot of help with painting, or building something, or whatever needed doing. Caryn's dad was a welder by trade, but he loved to make things with his hands. Mom never thought any of dad's hand made furniture was good enough to keep in their house. Luckily, he made a couple of pieces of furniture he gave to Caryn. Caryn still had them and kept them on display at her house. One was a curio cabinet, the other was a game table. Her father was never going to be able to make anymore furniture, since he was in a Alzheimer's care facility. Caryn's mom passed away several years ago. Even though her mother had been gone for years, it was her father that she missed the most.

Rob gave Caryn a big hug. Sometimes Rob felt that he was almost as gifted as Caryn, since Rob knew exactly what she was thinking. Jack and Ron turned around in their seats and thanked Caryn. Jack said they could not have done what Caryn did, and find Tom alive. Jack and Ron told Rob that they were going to keep Caryn's involvement out of the report. Caryn was now their "anonymous informant."

CHAPTER 21

Caryn gave a big sigh of relief. Tom was safe and so was her secret.

Jack handed Rob the evidence bag with the blanket inside. Jack looked at Caryn and said "I don't know how you do what you do. I don't know how tired you are after doing what you do, but can you do it again? Can you help us find this bastard?" When Rob handed the blanket, minus the bag, to Caryn, Rob hoped Caryn would get a vision of where the suspect was now. Caryn had told Rob that sometimes she got images from things she held in her hands, but it didn't always happen.

When Ron turned around to say something to Rob, Rob shook his head and motioned toward Caryn.

Jack then turned in his seat. They all sat waiting for Caryn to tell them what she was seeing.

After a couple of minutes, that felt like hours, Caryn finally looked to Rob and said "you have to stop him, he is following another little boy. He plans on tricking him too. He thinks Tom is going to be asleep for a while. But he doesn't plan on coming back here. He has heard the news about the police searching for Tom." Caryn then said, "he doesn't care if Tom is found or not. He thinks he is going to be long gone by the time Tom wakes up and goes for help."

Jack immediately radioed dispatch and asked them to broadcast an attempt to locate the light blue van, occupied by a male subject, wanted for kidnapping. Jack advised dispatch he would give more information shortly. When unkeyed his mic he asked Caryn about the suspect. Jack told Caryn he needed her help. Jack wanted to get this guy before he hurt anyone else. Caryn said she saw him as a while male adult. She said he appeared to be in his mid 40s because his hair was turning gray on the top and sides. He was clean shaven. Caryn then said "when he talked to Tom, he told Tom his name was John, but I felt he was lying to Tom, even about his name." Caryn then said she saw a tatoo on his arm. She said "I could see part of it. It's on his right arm. All I could see was the first two letters A and D. The rest of the tattoo was covered by the sleeve of his t-shirt.

Rob asked Caryn if she saw where the suspect was currently. Caryn said "I could see a movie theater marquis and the Truckee River." Rob turned to Jack and told him it sounded like the suspect was downtown. Caryn then said "his van is parked in the parking garage across the street from the theater. You better hurry because he is talking to a young boy."

Caryn told Rob, Jack and Ron that the boy was about the same age as Tom. She told them that the suspect told the boy that he wanted to see the new action movie that everyone was talking about. Caryn said "the boy just told the suspect that is the same movie he wants to see too. That's why he is standing outside the theater. He is hoping to sneak in but he is scared to try."

Caryn then said "the boy just told the suspect that he left his house without his parents permission. He wanted to see the movie but they told him they did not have enough money for the movies." Then Caryn tensed up and said "he just told the boy that he will take him to the movies, but he did not bring enough money for them both. He said he has to go home and get more money, but since he is closer to the Sparks theater, why doesn't the boy go with him, then they can both go to the Sparks theater together."

While Caryn was telling Rob, Jack was relaying all the information to the dispatcher. The dispatcher sent several units that were working downtown. Luckily the City of Reno added extra personnel during the high tourist times. This was one of those times. Some of the extra personnel were retired police officers, some retired from other agencies. They made extra money to add to their retirement, plus they felt they were an asset to the police department by assisting when they could. These officers only worked downtown, and worked a walking beat. That meant they did not have a vehicle. The police department was within easy walking distance of the downtown area.

Jack asked for any plain clothes detectives to respond to the downtown theater and look for the suspect and the boy. Jack wanted to make sure no other boy was placed in the same position that Tom was, fighting for his life.

Caryn told Jack that the boy was a white male juvenile, with reddish blonde hair. He was wearing levis shorts and a red t-shirt that was so long it almost completely covered the shorts. When Jack relayed the description of the boy, a bike officer (a police officer that patrolled downtown while riding a

10 speed bicycle) said he had just seen a boy matching that description talking to a "WMA". The bike officer told dispatch he would return, and advise where the subjects were. The dispatcher closed the radio frequency since she had an officer in the area, and they were attempting to

locate a suspect and a possible victim of a kidnapping. The officer radioed in that the male adult and juvenile were both walking towards the parking garage.

Jack asked the bike officer if he could stall them until the detectives and the other officers responding,could get into position. Jack knew there were a lot of people in that area, at any time of day or night. Jack did not want a hostage situation. Jack was sure that the suspect did not believe the Reno Police Department had narrowed their investigation. Jack believed the suspect thought the police department was attempting to locate a missing juvenile, not a kidnapping victim. But, Jack did not know if the suspect was armed. Jack knew now that everything Caryn had told them was accurate. But even Caryn could not say if the suspect had a weapon, or what his intentions to the boy were.

Two walking beat officers met up with the bike officer. One of the retired officers said he had to do something like this when he was with the Riverside Police Department. The officer said he made up a story about a missing toddler. The subject he was trying to separate from a possible victim told the officer he would help look for him. When the subject walked away, the officer grabbed the possible victim and pulled him to safety. The retired officer said, "since there are three of us, to the suspect it would look like we have begun a search. Lets try it." The bike officer radioed dispatch and told the dispatcher and the other units what they had planned. He told the other two officers that he would ride towards the river like he is in a hurry. The other two officers would walk up to the adult and juvenile and asked if they had seen a toddler alone.

The officer was thrilled when he asked both subjects if they had seen a two year old toddler, because the boy said he had seen a toddler walkingwith his mother about

20 minutes ago. The officer asked the boy if he could show him where. When the boy walked towards the river, with the officer, the male adult continued to walk towards the parking garage. When the suspect turned back and saw that the other officer was still watching him, he started to run. The bike officer radioed dispatch and told them that the boy was safe but the officers on scene were in foot pursuit of the suspect running towards the parking garage on Sierra St.

Jack had been driving towards the downtown area when he heard the update. Jack directed the closest detective unit (who was just arriving in the area) to block off the entrance to the parking garage.

With more officers arriving in the area, the suspect saw he had no where to run. Before any officer could get close to the suspect, he pulled a gun and shot himself in the chest. He died almost instantly.

Rob never did find out why Adam Barnes was abducting young boys, but something good did come out of it. Rob found out that a book author who lived in Nevada, was an expert in child safety. Rob contacted him after buying his books from a local book store. After Rob told Bob about the two boys, Tom and Sam (the name of the little boy from the downtown theater), he met with Rob and the boys and taught all of them all about "stranger danger." Rob was surprised that there were things that he didn't even know. Rob thought "thank God for people like Bob Kahn, who wrote such an important book "Bobby and Mandee's Too Safe for Strangers." Rob was surprised it wasn't a best seller. Every parent and teacher should have the book.

The boys enjoyed meeting the author, especially after they read the book. Rob thought it was too bad that the boys had not read the book before they became victims of a bad stranger. Then they would have known what to do. Rob told the parents of Tom and Sam to also read it. Rob and Bob were now friends and got together as often as their schedules allowed.

CHAPTER 22

Rob had to focus on what happened to the dispatch center and if it was an accident or intentional. While the fire department was still trying to determine what happened, the police department was investigating it as an act of terrorism. If it was intentional, he was going to find out who did it and then heaven help them. If anything happened to Caryn he did not know what he would do. Caryn was his whole world.

Rob knew the dispatch center was a secured area. Anyone who knew how to disable the entire communications center was going to be a tough adversary. The question was, how did they know how to disable the dispatch center?

Rob vowed the suspects should enjoy the time they had left because they didn't know that Rob was going to make them pay. After all, they had hurt the most important person in his life, his wife Caryn. Someone would pay. He would make sure of it. He was mad as Hell. And he was scared. That was not a good combination for the bad guy. Rob was going to be like a bull dog now. He would not let go. He prayed, "Please God, let Caryn be okay, and let me find the son of a bitch that did this to her. Let me have five minutes alone with him so I can explain to him, you don't mess with mine! "

Rob would follow protocol. He would play by the rules. After all he was a professional law enforcement officer for the "Biggest Little City in the World". Rob would make sure they paid, and paid dearly. But he would do it legally. Rob believed in the Justice System. If he didn't, he could not do the job he was being paid to do.

CHAPTER 23

When Rob got to the police station, he had to park two blocks away at the corners of Mill & High Street. He could not find a parking spot closer. He had to walk past several vehicles, some he had never seen before. He found out later that they belonged to ATF (Alcohol, Tobacco, and Firearms), FBI (Federal Bureau of Investigation), WCSO (Washoe County Sheriff's Office) AND SPD (Sparks Police Department), to name a few.

Rob ran the two blocks to the station. The Reno Police Department was located at the corner of Second Street and High Street. It was an ugly green building, three stories high. The 2nd floor used to be the old Reno jail, before they built the Washoe County Jail on Parr Blvd. Now all the people arrested, no matter if they were arrested by Sparks PD, NHP (Nevada Highway Patrol), WCSO (Washoe County Sheriff's Office), or RPD (Reno Police Department), got taken to the same jail. It used to be that Reno and Washoe County had separate jails. The new Washoe County Jail was built to accommodate hundreds of prisoners. But it turns out, it was not big enough. It was inadequate by the time it was completed.

Some people said the second floor of the Reno Police Department was haunted. One of the stories Rob heard was that a prisoner, wrongfully arrested for murder, was trying to escape. The man figured if he tied a bed sheet around the top rung of the cell door, it would look like he was trying to commit suicide. He would pretend he was unconscious. They would rush in, he would jump up, rush out, slam the door behind him and escape. What he didn't realize was, when they rushed in, they slammed the jail door against his head, crushing his skull, killing him instantly. Of course the coroner found him laying on the floor of the cell, the sheet still tied around his neck, with a skull fracture. It happened in 1934, when reports were not as detailed and investigations were not as involved. The coroner, seeing the sheet around his neck, said "suicide." Case closed.

It was said the ghost walked the 2nd floor, looking for an escape, so he could prove his innocence. No one had seen him. But everyone swore they felt extremely cold when they got into a certain area of the 2nd floor. Rob's office was in that area of the police station. He didn't believe in ghosts. Rob believed there was a draft somewhere. Rob had not found it yet, but he swore he would find it eventually.

CHAPTER 24

Rob jogged into the lobby and could not believe the amount of people who were there. Unfortunately, most of them were the press. Rob sympathized with them. He knew they had a job to do, just like he did. It was too bad that Rob's job conflicted with theirs. Rob passed them, not saying anything. Rob punched in the code and walked through the secured door and down the hall to the Chief's Office. To the left of the office was the conference room. It's this room where the Chief of Police had his meetings because it could seat twenty people comfortably. Rob looked in, but no one was there. He walked back to the Chief's Desk and called the lobby. A very harried sounding lady answered the phone. Rob asked, "where is the Chief?" When she was hesitant to tell him, he identified himself. She took a big gulp of air and said, "I've never talked to you before, how do I know you are who you say you are?"

Rob was feeling the pressure by now, not to mention just a little uptight, so he started to yell. But then he stopped. He knew everyone was scared for their fellow employees in the basement of a building that no one could enter. Rob apologized and gave his identification number so she could verify who he was. She thanked him and told him the chief was in the briefing room.

The briefing room was used when police officers coming on duty were briefed on where the problem areas were, what crimes were committed, what officer was working what area of the city, and what bad guys to look for. Rob knew that briefing could contain from twenty-five to sixty officers depending on what shift was coming on duty.

Rob looked at his watch. It was 0835 hours. Graveyard shift had gotten off work at 0800 hours (8:00 a.m.). Day shift came on duty at 0700 hours (7:00 a.m.). Rob wondered what the Chief was doing. Was he holding another briefing? Is that why there were so many cars parked around the station?

The closer Rob came to the briefing room, the louder the voices. There were approximately thirty-five people inside the room. Rob recognized some of them because he had worked with them. Charlie, from ATF (Alcohol, Tobacco, and Firearms) Doug, with the FBI (Federal Bureau of Investigations). Roger, was a Lieutenant with the Sparks Police Department. It turned out that employees from all over the state of Nevada, were here to volunteer their services. There were even a few were from Northern California. Some were dispatchers who volunteered to answer phone calls when they were not working for their own agencies. Rob never thought the brotherhood had extended that far. Rob, even as concerned about Caryn as he was, could not help feel the emotional pride in these people. They were all here to help.

Chief William Williams was explaining something that was not going over too well. Rob stood in the back of the room.

Chief Williams had not seen Rob come in yet. The Chief was explaining that the fire department had closed off the building until the Hazardous Materials Unit had cleared the scene and said it was okay to go in. The fire department had the experience and expertise and no one could over ride their decisions. Everyone had to wait. Including the Reno Police Department. No one knew what had happened, until the fire department gave the okay to investigate the scene of the crime.

Hazardous Materials crews were in there right now. They had notified personnel on scene that all four dispatchers were unconscious. Alive, but unconscious. They had all the dispatchers hooked up to oxygen getting them stabilized so they could be transported to the hospital. The Hazardous Materials personnel had to make sure the dispatchers did not have to be quarantined. The fire department had to follow protocol. They could not place anyone else in jeopardy. If they had contracted a deadly disease, they would have to be treated where they were, until provisions were made for them to be in an isolated environment. No one could talk to the dispatchers until the hazmat units were sure that what happened to the dispatchers was an isolated incident.

Approximately 20 minutes later the police chief was notified that the dispatchers were all coming around. All except one. She was still unconscious. The fire department hazmat crew said it did not look good. The Chief caught Rob's eye. Rob could see how this news affected him. The chief could not imagine how it was affecting Rob.

Oh God! Rob thought. Please, don't let it be Caryn. I don't want anyone to suffer, but please let Caryn be okay.

CHAPTER 25

The Chief was trying to keep the news positive, without saying much. Chief Williams knew that if the media doesn't receive answers, they speculate and put a "spin" on their own stories. Right now they were doing a wonderful job of that. The news stories circulating was, a foreign government practiced with an unknown type weapon on Reno. Their next target would be the United States Capital. Rumor was also spreading that Reno was not the only city it happened to. It also happened to Las Vegas, Nevada; Portland, Oregon; and Seattle Washington. Chief Williams, by now, was getting desperate for news. They had to get the dispatchers out.

Finally, after three more hours, the blood tests came back, showing that the dispatchers were not contagious. They did not have an infectious disease. The air samples showed a high trace of an anesthetic that causes instant unconsciousness. The firemen, wearing their oxygen masks, carrying the breathing apparatus tanks on their backs, wearing their heavy turn outs, carrying stretchers, went into the dispatch center and removed all the dispatchers.

There were barricades to keep out the press and the public. But, there was still a large crowd that congregated behind the barricades. A loud cheer went out when the dispatchers were brought out on the stretchers. There were so many people standing in the streets, the barricades had to be moved to allow the ambulances to move into the parking lot, to take the first and second dispatchers away to the nearest hospital. The dispatchers could not hear the cheering, they were still unconscious.

One officer overheard a conversation between two women who were standing at the barricades closest to him. One woman made the comment "about a month ago I called to report a prowler in my yard. I live alone and I was so scared. When I called 911, the dispatcher I talked to was so kind and sweet. She reminded me of my daughter. She told me there were officers on their way to my house. She said if I heard anything to let her know. I didn't hear anything and told her it could have been my imagination. She said the officers would rather check it out and have it be nothing, than I not call, and have it be something. That sweet woman calmed me down, and listened to me tell her about my life. By the time the officers had arrived, checked out my vehicle, front and back yards and were knocking on my door, I felt safe and secure. She told me her name was Caryn. I hope she's not one of the injured dispatchers. I didn't get a chance to tell her how much I enjoyed talking to her, and to thank her for doing such a good job in a manner that kept me from being scared. She made me feel that my call was more important than a frightened woman who jumps at shadows."

CHAPTER 26

As the dispatchers got to the hospital, they were examined by doctors who had been standing by.

Caryn was being examined by a doctor when the blood tests returned, showing Caryn was pregnant. A gynecologist was called in to make sure the fetus had not been damaged. The doctor examined Caryn and said Caryn was 8 weeks pregnant. The fetus was all right.

Rob rushed in when the doctors were walking out of Caryn's room. Rob told them he was Caryn's husband and asked how she was doing. They told him Caryn and her baby were doing just fine.

Rob was shocked. He knew that Caryn did not know she was pregnant. If she had, she would have told Rob, so they could both celebrate. Heaven knows, they had tried for several years but there had been no baby. Rob and Caryn discussed adopting a baby.

Rob was thinking back to two months ago. Caryn had gotten off work the same time Rob did. That usually didn't happen. Rob remembered feeling like they were 2 ships passing each other, never knowing when they were going to pass each other again. Caryn waited for Rob to pick her up. When they got into the elevator, they looked at each other and knew they could not wait another minute to hold each other. To kiss each other. To make love to each other. Rob felt like it had been years since he had shown Caryn how much he loved her and needed her in his life. Rob hit the stop button of the elevator. He kissed Caryn until they were both senseless. Before he knew it, they were both undressed. Rob laid Caryn on top of their clothes, touching her all over. Kissing her all over. Rob loved the way Caryn came alive in his arms. He would never compare Sally and Caryn, but Rob knew he was loved by Caryn. She told him with her responses to his lovemaking. Sally always seemed to be in a hurry when they made love. Rob was always amazed how fast Caryn became so warm and loving. He saw her at work, and she was always very cool and professional. But when he touched her intimately, she moaned and pleaded with Rob not to stop. Of course, the last thing on Rob's mind was to stop. Rob mounted Caryn and with one thrust he was inside her warm body. Caryn came instantly. Before she was finished with one orgasm, another one came shortly after that.

That's when Rob came, moaning and crying out Carny's name. Rob kissed Caryn over and over again. Then Rob stood up, helped Caryn up and they both got dressed. Then Rob pushed the up button, waited for the elevator to arrive on the Lobby floor. Caryn and Rob, still holding hands walked out of the elevator and to Rob's car. Rob knew that was a very special time, and every time he rode the elevator, he remembered it. That always brought a smile to his face. Rob now realized that every time he rode the elevator at the fire station, to go to the dispatch center, he would remember the night his child was conceived. What a story he could tell his grand children.

Rob walked into the room and thought, he was the luckiest man alive. Not only did he have the most beautiful, wonderful wife, but he was going to be a father too. And they were both going to be okay.

He was going to get the bastards that had jeopardized his family. He would make sure they paid for what they did.

CHAPTER 27

Tommy knew it was too late for second thoughts. Dave said it would go down like clock work, and it did. With George's help, At 0420 hours (4:20 a.m.) they set off the chemical that would knock out dispatch. Then they went to the first casino, the Silver Slipper. There are no clocks in casinos. The owners of the casinos keep all distractions to a minimum. There are no windows and all the doors are closed. The doors remain unlocked but their closed. The casino floor of the Silver Slipper was a large open room, at the least the size of a football field. At peak time it could easily hold 500 people. All of them spending money, hoping to hit it big. Renoites knew that the elaborate casino owners hadn't built their big beautiful buildings because they paid off more than they brought in. At 4 am there were still approximately 200 people gambling at the tables and slot machines. The chemical that was used was fast acting. In less than three minutes, everyone was unconscious, either fallen to the floor or slumped over the tables.

What Tommy did not know at the time, and was not going to find out very soon was, he was a mass murderer. Because some of the chemical, some of the people had had heart attacks or the chemical affected their breathing. Whatever the reason, several people died that day. Tommy would be surprised to learn that so far the count was seventy-eight dead, and growing. No one knew what happened. It would not be discovered until 0730 hours (7:30 a.m.) when day shift would come to relieve the graveyard shift.

Tommy's brother, Gary, and three members of their gang, hit the Platinum Club at 0445 hours (4:45 a.m.). With Charlie's help, it went perfect. The back packs they had with them held the chemicals which were stored in small cylinders. They just opened the cylinders that were left in the back packs. They put on their gas masks while they were in the bathroom. Everyone was so involved in their gambling that no one knew what hit them. Of course the surveillance cameras picked up everything, but Charlie who worked in the security office, took care of that. He also took all the money in the vault while Gary and the others took the money from the change carts. Tommy was also taking money from the gamblers laying on the floor of the Silver Slipper. While Tommy was doing that he saw something so beautiful he had to have it. It was the most beautiful diamond ring he had ever seen. It was on the finger of an old lady who had passed out from the chemical.

When he picked up her hand it was cold. Tommy thought she was not used to the air conditioning that kept her skin so cold. It never occurred to him that she was dead. He never thought that anyone would die from the chemical. After all, they had taken the cylinders from a doctor's office. Tommy told himself "doctors don't keep chemicals around that hurt anyone." Gary told Tommy that no one would be hurt. Tommy vowed he would never take part in anything that hurt someone.

CHAPTER 28

Gary and the boys walked away with, what they figured was approximately a little over two million dollars. After the split, Gary figured that Tommy and him would not get as much but even if they only got one million dollars, that would be okay. With the money that was being taken from the bank, Gary was hoping they would have approximately 8 million dollars.

Scott was helping Tommy at the Silver Slipper. Scott wasn't as naive as Tommy. When Scott and the rest of the guys were removing cash and jewelry from their victims, Scott noticed that a few of the victims were not breathing. Scott swore to himself. Gary said the chemical would not hurt anyone. Scott did not want to go to the gas chamber, but it was too late now to worry about it. At least Scott would have enough money to take him anywhere in the world. He could live comfortably for the rest of his life. He thought "I shouldn't be held accountable for something I did not know would happen."

Joe, Steve and Rich were just leaving the First National Bank branch in the Wedge Plaza. It was located at Wedge Parkway and the Mount Rose Highway. The plaza had approximately 10 stores. Most of them were small "mom and pop" places. But, there was a large grocery store and a bank. The front of the bank was all windows, including the front door. All the glass windows and door were alarmed. They smashed in the front door by driving through it with the push bar of their pick up truck.

They knew the alarm had gone off and the alarm company was calling the Washoe County Sheriffs Department Dispatch Center. They also knew no one at the dispatch center would be answering the phones for a while. They ran into the bank, ran to the vault, blew off the door with dynamite. The sound of the explosion was muffled, but they didn't care if it was a loud noise.

They knew that no one lived in the area for at least a couple of miles. And if anyone called to report an explosion, again no one would answer the phone at the dispatch center. When they got into the vault, they put all the money and the safety deposit boxes into large green garbage bags that they put into the back of their camper. They were laughing with glee when they realized they were literally walking away with millions of dollars.

While Joe, Steve and Rich were removing money from the First National Bank south of Reno, Lenny and Mark were removing money from the Security National Bank, that was located north of Reno.

They did the same thing, driving a truck with a camper. The Security National Bank was isolated. It was on the corner of Lemon Valley Drive and Patrician, in Lemon Valley. There were houses nearby, but again, even if anyone heard the alarm go off and called it in, no one in the dispatch center was awake to answer the call or send someone to investigate.

CHAPTER 29

R ob was just pulling into the parking lot of the police station when he heard the alert tones go off on the radio. Apparently the alternate emergency dispatch center was now manned by radio dispatchers that had been called into work. Or the off duty dispatchers came to help after hearing about what was going on. One thing about the job, there was a camaraderie that you couldn't find anywhere else.

The tones on the radio indicated an emergency. As soon as Rob heard the dispatcher's voice on the radio, he knew it was going to be very very bad. Robin's voice was shaking. Robin was a very good dispatcher and Rob trusted her to do her job and keep him and all his fellow officers safe. More important, Caryn trusted her. And Caryn should know since she worked with Robin. Rob knew that Robin had handled a lot of emergencies. Her voice never revealed the stress she was under. Until now. She called out a trouble unknown, several subjects down, several code 50's (dead bodies). The call was at the Platinum Club which was located at Second Street and Lake Street.

Rob knew The Platinum Club was a very ritzy establishment. Rob had received info that the Platinum Club had four million dollars on hand for the high rollers coming into town for Kool Klassic Nights. Now Rob knew what the motive was. What the reason was to disable the dispatchers by rendering them unconscious. The City of Reno had been robbed.

A short time later Rob heard the tones go off again. The second time the alert tones were activated, Rob knew that another casino must have been robbed. He was right. It was the Silver Slipper. It wasn't as nice as the Platinum Club but it was a larger casino. Rob did not know how much money on hand they had, but it had to have been at least a million dollars.

Rob heard the on duty sergeant request that all the local hospitals, Saint Mary's and Washoe Medical Center, be placed on stand by. There were the people from the Silver Slipper and the Platinum Club. Plus the other emergencies that were routine for any hospital.

The PIO (Public Information Officer) was fending off all calls from the news agencies all over the United States.

From the governor of Nevada, to the man next door, they were all asking how something this bad, this heinous, could happen, and no one was aware of it happening until it was all over?

The television news anchors were asking all the police departments around the nation "if it can happen in Reno, Nevada, can it happen in your city?"

CHAPTER 30

All of the suspects had arranged to meet at the Barge Inn, a low rent motel on West Fourth Street. The motel was really very small cabins. It was the perfect location. Isolated cabins that no one would care what was going on as long as the rent was paid. The Barge Inn was six miles east of the California State Line. It was off of Highway Interstate 80.

There were only 9 cabins. Most of the time they were rented on a weekly or monthly basis. Gary had stayed in cabin #9 when he first moved to Reno. When he called the manager of the Barge Inn, the manager told Gary he was in luck. The weekly renter had died recently and the manager had just finished cleaning out cabin #9. Gary felt it was an indication that things were finally going to keep going his way. Cabin #9 was a 3 room cabin with a double bed, a kitchen (if you could call it that) consisting of a sink, 2 burner stove and a very small refrigerator. The last room was a bathroom consisting of a sink, toilet and bath tub/shower combination, minus the shower curtain. The cabin interior was painted a pukey green. The paint was peeling. It even smelled as if someone had gotten sick, and whoever cleaned the room could not get rid of the smell. Tommy thought the color matched the smell. "Pukey". Tommy wasn't sure how many colors were underneath. He could see blue, pink, yellow, dirty white and maybe a striped wall paper.

Wherever the paint was peeling, he could see a different color. It looked like it was painted every time they got a new tenant.

Tommy, Gary and the boys were going to meet here, stay two nights, then divvy up the loot. George and Charlie would arrive later that afternoon. Each one would get their fair share and drive to California. Each of them would open up a bank account and then spend a little money in California. They would then leave the country, taking a cashier's check for the balance of their money. No one would know where the money came from. If they had to, they would open more than one account.

Even if they had a television or radio in the cabin, none of them thought about listening to it. They were caught up in counting the money, jewelry, and anything else of value. If Tommy had, he would have found out that the reason his girlfriend had not called him or returned his calls was because she was still unconscious. And no one knew if she would ever regain consciousness.

CHAPTER 31

When Rob found out that the same anesthesia gas used on the dispatchers was used in the Platinum Club and the Silver Slipper, Rob became pissed off all over again. Rob swore he would get the son of a bitch behind it all.

He owed this to Caryn! He hadn't protected her like he promised to, the day he married her.

Chief Williams was going to have a press conference later in the day. The Chief just found out that the suspects used some type of gas to knock out the dispatchers. The gas was pumped through an air vent that led from the outside of the fire station, directly down into the basement, where the dispatch center was. The chief remembered that he had received several complaints. They had been made by the dispatch staff. Especially when an off duty fireman had parked his vehicle near the vent and left the vehicle running. The exhaust fumes gave the on duty dispatchers head aches because of the carbon monoxide. But Chief Williams thought he had taken care of the problem. He had sent every city employee a copy of a memo that directed the employees not to park there anymore.

When the news came through that the Silver Slipper, the Platinum Club and two banks had been robbed, the Chief could not believe it. This was the busiest time of the year. There were literally hundreds of thousands of tourists in Reno. Chief Williams knew that a lot of money the City of Reno needed to keep the city running, came from tourists and special events. The chief thought it couldn't get any worse than this. But he was wrong.

The chief was told that seventy-eight people were dead from the gas that was used. Thirty-three more were not expected to live. Two hundred and fourteen were recovering. The ones recovering had a fifty-fifty chance of a full recovery. The ones that did not fully recover would have respiratory problems for the rest of their lives.

CHAPTER 32

Chief Williams was just hanging up the phone when the City Manager and four City Councilmen swooped in. The Chief thought, "great, just what I needed in this fucked up day!" The City Manager, John Foster, was a perfect politician. He was an asshole to every one who would not kiss his feet, or could not make him look good. He especially did not like bad publicity.

Chief Williams had come from a large department back east. Bill Williams applied for the chief of police job after seeing it advertised in a law enforcement magazine he had a subscription to. Chief Williams thought a change of scene would help his marriage. They weren't as close they should have been, married as long as they were. His wife Ann, and him, would be celebrating their 43rd wedding anniversary next month. Chief Williams had always thought the move to Reno was a good one. His wife, Sue, enjoyed Reno. She wasn't a gambler but she told him, "Bill, I go to the casino to watch the people." Now he wasn't so sure he had made the right move, coming to Reno. He thought, "were all city managers pricks, or am I the only unlucky police chief to have to deal with an arrogant son of a bitch?"

John expected miracles. He expected the chief to have the suspects in custody by the end of the day. John did not want the publicity to hurt his chances of not receiving his usual cash bonus for a job well done. No other city employee received a bonus but John knew he was too important to the city not to get one. After all, didn't he tell the city council at every meeting that if it wasn't for him, the City of Reno wouldn't be as popular as it was. Granted, Kool Klassic Nights started long before he came to Reno, but he kept it going year after year. He made sure it was bigger and better every year. Maybe there was more crime than years before, but you had to take the good with the bad. Just like a typical paranoid would think, "it's not my fault."

Having several people die was no concern to John Foster, but—having two casinos who had supported John Foster's appointment to the position of City Manager, was. That meant the Chief was treated like shit. John Foster had no sympathy for the chief. After all, the chief was making them all look bad. So he treated the chief like crap. Like something John Foster would wipe off his shoes, before he would walk in the door.

Rob found out the drug used was a form of chloroform. It was an odorless gas that knocked everyone out, almost immediately. The ones who died were either allergic to the gas, had weak hearts, or the altitude change coming to Reno had affected their hearts. Like the doctor explained, it was too much—too fast. The question Rob was asking himself was, "where did they get it from?" And, "did they know there were side effects of the drug. Deadly side effects."

CHAPTER 33

Tommy had been sent out to buy food. He didn't mind going. It would take his mind off Carla. Tommy was concerned because hadn't gotten a page or a text from Carla, letting him know what was going on. It had been prearranged that Carla would text or page him when she was awake and alone. They both knew that the gas had to affect Carla to make it look like she was unaware of what was happening. It was only going to affect the dispatchers for a few hours. Tommy and Carla had it figured out that within 48 hours Carla would be able to have some time alone. Even if she did not have the ability to text or page him, she could use the hospital phone to call him on his cell phone. She would pretend that she was talking to her brother, just in case the phones were being monitored. By the time anyone checked, and found out she was an only child, she would be long gone. With Tommy.

While standing at the check out stand, waiting to pay for the groceries he saw a local newspaper. His mouth hung open in shock when he saw the headlines. He could not believe what he was reading. People died from the gas that Tommy had used. PEOPLE HAD DIED!!! Not only one or two, not even ten or twenty. The count was up to one hundred and two. Tommy prayed that Carla was not one of them But, Tommy thought, how would he find out? He bought the newspaper hoping they would have a list of names, praying he did not see Carla's. There was a local phone number listed for anyone who had information regarding the heinous crime that had occurred. The phone number could also be called if they wanted to know if a relative or loved one was a victim.

Tommy rushed to the pay phone outside. He did not know that all calls were taped, and all calls had caller ID showing where the calls were coming from. Anyone giving false information was immediately checked. Tommy called from the pay phone outside the Albertson store. When the officer answered the phone and asked where Tommy was calling from, Tommy said he was calling from out of state. The officer, never hesitating or making Tommy cautious, flagged down another officer to pick up the line and had dispatch send units to the pay phone. This was the first break they had had all day. The officer was going to keep Tommy on the phone as long as he possibly could. Officer Jackson was glad he could help, but damn, he wanted to go to that pay phone and punch the idiot out for what had happened to not only the citizens and tourists of Reno.

He was pissed off that anyone would mess with his dispatchers. He knew dispatchers felt that the officers, deputies and firemen belonged to them. He wondered if they knew the men and women who worked with them, felt the same way about the dispatchers. They did a tough job, in a lousy work environment without getting much support from the front lines. This time, they had put their lives on the line. This officer was only too glad to help bring the scum bags in.

Rob was in his car, coming back from the hospital, when he was called on the radio. Because Rob was the lead investigator, they notified him. The dispatcher told Rob that a suspicious phone call had been received asking about one of the injured dispatchers. Rob asked where the call originated from. They told him it was from one of the pay phones outside the Albertson store at Fourth Street and Keystone Avenue. Rob told the dispatcher he would be responding. He asked for a couple of detective units to assist him. He also asked for two patrol units in case they needed marked patrol units to stop the possible suspect.

When Rob drove up he noticed a man inside the phone booth. The man looked to be about 29 years old, white, male, six foot one inch tall, brownish blonde hair. What Rob was surprised to see about the man was the panic the man showed on his face. Rob told dispatch he was going to contact a possible suspect. Rob did not know if the man was armed but Rob considered him armed and very dangerous.

Tommy had his back to the parking lot to cut down on the noise. Rob told dispatch to close the frequency and waited until the first marked police unit arrived. Rob had the two detectives and one patrol unit more officers park out of sight of the phone booth. Rob wanted to make sure the guy was alone. He asked dispatch for two other officers to block the entrances to the parking lot. Rob decided if the suspect was armed, Rob did not want any more innocent people be killed by this fucking madman.

Rob swore if anyone was going to be killed it would be the suspect. Rob was so mad to think that this man had hurt so many people, including his precious wife and unborn child. When everyone was in position, approximately five minutes later, Rob approached the phone booth with his service weapon drawn.

Tommy had been put on hold, waiting while the police officer checked his list of victims. He told Tommy that the list was extensive because all the names were written on several sheets of paper. And they were not in alphabetical order. Tommy turned around when someone knocked on the door of the pay phone. Tommy turned around to tell the asshole knocking on the door that the asshole would just have to wait. His was an important phone call. Instead, when he turned around, he saw a hundred police officers (it was only three—but with all of them armed with guns and the guns pointed at him—who counts or cares?) All of the officers looked very mad. Tommy knew he was the reason they were pissed off. And Tommy knew they had a right to be.

CHAPTER 34

Rob read Tommy his rights and asked Tommy if he understood them. All Tommy could do was stand there and stare at all the guns pointed at him. After Tommy finally pulled it together, he told Rob, "yeah, I got it." Rob told Tommy that a terrorist act had damaged the communications center and robbed and killed several people in two casinos. Rob had knowledge that Tommy had been involved.

Tommy blurted out, "is Carla okay?" Rob asked Tommy who Carla was. Tommy told Rob that Carla was his girlfriend who was also a police dispatcher for the Reno Police Department. Rob realized Tommy was talking about Carla Anderson. Rob asked one of the police officers to go to Washoe Medical Center and stand guard over Dispatcher Carla Anderson, until Rob could determine if she was an accomplice or an unfortunate victim.

Rob knew that Carla was still in a coma. Carla had been affected worse than any of the others. All the other dispatchers were conscious but still feeling the effects of the gas. Carla had not regained consciousness and the doctors were not real hopeful for a complete recovery. Caryn and her fellow dispatchers were all worried about Carla. Rob told Tommy that Carla was in serious condition. The doctors were not sure what else they could do because they were not sure what drug had been used. Tommy started to cry.

Carla was the love of his life. If it hadn't been for his brother, and the contact person his brother got all the information from, Carla would be just fine. Tommy was so mad, he told Rob everything. The only thing he could not tell Rob was, what gas was used, and who the inside person was at the police department.

Rob drove to the District Attorney's Office with Tommy's taped confession. Rob got a search warrant for the Barge Inn. Tommy told Rob that the rest of the suspects were waiting for Tommy to return. Unfortunately, the contact person Tommy had mentioned was monitoring the radio. He heard Tommy was in custody.

He left his office and drove to the pay phone in front of the seven-eleven store at the corner of Second Street and Wells Avenue. He called Gary on the phone. He told them they had Tommy in custody and that Rob went to the District Attorney's Office for a search warrant. The contact person did not know that five officers had been sent to the Barge Inn, to stake out cabin nine, until Rob arrived with the warrant. Gary was unaware that the Reno Police Department had so much information, courtesy of his brother Tommy. The officers were to monitor all traffic in and out, and let Rob know how many people were in cabin number nine.

Rob was just leaving the District Attorney's Office when one of the officers called him. He said a gray van had just arrived. Two people got out and exited the vehicle. The officer told Rob, they looked all around, then opened the back doors and unloaded at least ten large packing boxes. Three more people came out of the cabin to help them unload it. Then a sixth guy came running out and all the guys started putting the same boxes back and took out more boxes from the cabin to put in the van.

Officer Don MacDonald, Mac to his friends, told

Rob the boxes were obviously loaded with something heavy because it took two guys to carry the larger boxes. And they looked heavy.

Rob told Mac that he had the search warrant. Rob also said he was calling out SWAT (SPECIAL WEAPONS ASSAULT TEAM). Tommy told Rob that some of the gang carried handguns hidden on their body. Also, that they may have some dynamite left over, after they robbed the two banks. Mac told Rob that the manager was contacted and all other cabins had been evacuated.

Rob told Mac to close off the entrance/exit to the Barge Inn. Rob called dispatch on his cell phone. He asked them to call the SWAT Commander and have them meet him at the corner of Fourth Street and McCarran Boulevard. He did not want any radio traffic because the suspects may have a scanner. And because someone Rob worked with was also a suspect. They had all sworn to uphold the law. They had sworn to protect and serve the citizens and visitors of Reno. They had promised to keep the city safe. But one of them lied. The problem was, who was the son-of-a- bitch?

CHAPTER 35

It went better than Rob expected. Swat had surrounded cabin #9 and had turned off all the utilities. After the first sixteen hours, the suspects ran out of food. When the electricity and water was shut off, the suspects lasted another four hours in 100+ degrees heat. They finally gave up. When they came out, they smelled so bad, they could not stand to be by each other. The thought of being stuck in the cabin one more minute would have started them killing each other. Rob didn't think that would have been a bad idea, but he needed to know who the master mind was.

After giving them their Miranda Warnings, none of them talked. They all agreed to remain silent. Now that Rob had all the bad guys in custody, he figured the only thing left to do was see all of these people in court.

Rob decided the inside person, at the Reno Police Department, was Carla. It made sense. She worked in dispatch. She knew there was no fail safe system in place in case dispatch lost phones or power. Carla knew if the alarm companies tried to call the police dispatch center, but did not get an answer, they would just retry a few minutes later. Most, if not all alarm companies only monitored the alarm systems they installed. They did not send anyone out to check it first. They called the police department or the sheriff's

99

department, through the dispatch center. Rob had her in custody under guard, even though she was still unconscious.

However, after questioning Gary, Rob realized that Tommy was right after all. Tommy's brother, Gary, slipped when he said, "you didn't get all of us, one of the guys got away!" Rob thought, "I missed one? I was so damned sure I got them all!"

After talking to Tommy again, he found out that Tommy had overheard a conversation Gary had with someone on the phone, just before the attack on dispatch. The guy was someone Gary knew. Gary never said what his name was. He just said to the guy "your the boss!"

Gary was brought in again to the interview room. Gary refused to say anything until Rob told them they had counted all the money and approximately two million dollars was unaccounted for. Gary became very quiet. His face started to turn red.

With a very cold voice he said "that son-of-a- bitch". Gary looked at Rob and said, "I don't know what his name is. He told us to call him chief. He said he was going to be the next Chief of Police for the city of Reno. I know he's a Reno Police officer, and has rank, but I don't know what it is."

Rob was speechless. An officer of the law could do this? He hadn't thought so, but now that he thought about it, it was too well planned out. Rob couldn't fathom someone he worked with, someone he trusted with his life to do this. But they had. They had literally gotten away with murder. They had hurt hundreds of innocent people. This man had jeopardized the lives of men and women who were his lifeline on the radio. Who were his co-workers.

He had hurt the radio dispatchers who were always there. Who always monitored the radio, answered phone calls from citizens reporting everything and anything. They worked in the basement of a building. The same building that had caused them to put their lives on the line. And for what? For some asshole who had visions of greatness. An asshole who did not care about other people, about the badge he wore, or about the citizens of Reno he had sworn to protect. Rob swore he would get the bastard. No one was going to make a mockery of the Reno Police Department. The people, men and women Rob worked with, were the best. They were caring and dedicated. And now, God help them, one of them was a murderer.

Rob went straight to the Chief. He could not follow chain of command and go to his Lieutenant. What if the Lieutenant was the murderer? What if the Deputy Chief was the murderer? He knew Chief Williams was not the murderer because the suspect, told Gary he was going to be the next Chief of Police. When Rob talked to Chief Williams, the Chief said some not very nice words then said, "get him, any way you have to, get him! Report directly to me. I want this guy. I want him to pay for what he did."

Rob figured, whoever was the mastermind, had $2,000.000. and that he had to do something with it. Rob was afraid the asshole now knew Gary and the rest of the suspects were in custody. Would be rabbit? Rob also knew the suspect had some rank, and was very ambitious. Would he be able to get away with this? Did he have something else planned? Did he plan on killing the Chief of Police expecting to take his place? Rob believed that the suspect would be leaving. He had to hide the money. He had to know that Rob and the entire police department would be looking for him. Rob would not give up. Rob asked Chief Williams for the list of the sergeants and above, who when they called in sick, said they would be out for at least three days. Rob looked at the list. On all shifts, two lieutenants and three sergeants had called in sick. The two lieutenants had stated they would be back the next day. Rob would check on them last. He checked the three sergeants first. Out of the three sergeants, there was only one who said he would be out the rest of the week.

That sergeant was none other than the asshole who used to be the Lieutenant in charge of dispatch. He was the lieutenant that Rob's ex-wife left him for. Rob thought, "this would be too easy." I would definitely love to see this guy the suspect but I'm biased. I want this bastard to be the son of a bitch I've been looking for. Rob decided to check out all the other lieutenants and sergeants first. Then if they all checked out, he would go with his gut instinct and bring the bastard down.

Rob checked the two sergeants on the list and found out both of them had been working almost non stop. Because they had worked almost 20 hours out of the 24 hour day, they both got very ill. One of them had pneumonia and the other had the chicken pox that he got from his daughter. Both lieutenants also checked out okay. That meant Rob was right. But now what was he going to do. Rob decided he would tell Chief Williams. He went to the Chief and told him who he thought the suspect was. Chief Williams, knowing Rob's history, asked Rob if he could act impartially when he took the suspect into custody. Chief Williams told Rob that everything had to be done "by the book." Rob answered as honestly as he could. He would bring him down legally any way he could. He did not hold a grudge because of his ex-wife. Rob knew if his ex wife had not left, Rob would never have married Caryn and would not be a father-to-be now.

But, Rob told the chief "I will bring him in. He will answer to what he has done. He has shamed the uniform that he

wore. He will live to regret that." Chief Williams was satis-
fied with the answer and called the SWAT Commander at
home. The Chief told the Commander that there was going
to be a meeting in his office in 30 minutes. Chief Williams
expected all SWAT members to be there in full gear. The
SWAT Commander had kept his team on full alert since the
dispatchers had been found unconscious. Commander Judy
Hoskins expected to be called out and told her team to be
ready. To be able to respond at a moment's notice.

CHAPTER 36

When the meeting began, Chief Williams explained to his troops that he was going to send them on a call-out, that in their wildest dreams they never imagined they would ever be called out for. The Chief was sending them to take down one of their own sergeants. A Sergeant that they had all worked with at one time or another. The SWAT guys were a little apprehensive, but they all respected the Chief and Rob. If Rob's investigation had concluded that this Sergeant was the last suspect outstanding, that was good enough for them. They could not imagine anyone at work could so callously put a co-worker in jeopardy.

Rob again, went to the District Attorney's Office armed with all the documentation he needed to get the search warrant for Sergeant Mark Mills, with the Reno Police Department. Rob obtained the warrant with no fuss at all (Chief Williams had called the district attorney while Rob had been en-route). The SWAT guys had responded to the Sergeant's house and had set up a perimeter. All sides of the house were covered.

Now, someone had to make sure the Sergeant was in the house. One of the female officers, making herself sound like she was in dispatch, called and gave the Sergeant a message to call the Chief about an upcoming assignments. The Sergeant had answered the phone on the eighth ring, sounding out of breath. The officer joked with him, asking if he was doing something he shouldn't be. The Sergeant said his doctor told him he needed a vacation and that he was going away for a week. When the officer asked where, he was vague, saying he was going camping in the great outdoors. Officer Sue Collins, after hanging up the phone, relayed to Rob what had transpired. Rob felt he was running out of time. Rob just hoped the phone call did not alert Mark that he had been found out.

CHAPTER 37

Rob called to let Chief Williams know that Sergeant Mills was home, but may not be for long. Rob told Chief Williams that he had to contact the Sparks Police Department, because Sergeant Mills lived in Sparks. Rob discussed with the Chief what equipment and manpower would be needed.

Rob suggested that not only would the SWAT Team be necessary, he also recommended the fire department send a Hazmat Response Team. Rob remembered seeing all the dispatchers unconscious from a gas that Sergeant Mills may still be in possession of.

Chief Williams called the Sparks Police Chief. Chief Johnson said his department was at the disposal of the Reno Police Department, and would help in any way they could. After the call, Chief Johnson notified the patrol watch commander.

The Sparks Police Department Watch Commander, Lieutenant Morgan, could understand what the officers and staff of the Reno Police Department was feeling. He knew how he would feel if it was an officer with the Sparks Police Department. He knew that they were only human, but he always liked to think the men and women he worked with, took their jobs, and their oath of office very seriously. He contacted two detectives who immediately responded to

Sergeant Mills' house. Sergeant Mills lived two blocks north of the Sparks Police Department. He lived in a newer residential area. Since it was a newer area, quite a few of the homes were still unoccupied. Lieutenant Morgan knew Sergeant Mills personally. Lieutenant Morgan had never liked him and always thought it was a personality conflict, or it was Sgt. Mills' attitude that he was better than anybody else. Lieutenant Morgan always felt uncomfortable around Sergeant Mills. Now he knew why. Sergeant Mills was a corrupt police officer who was giving all officials a bad name. Lieutenant Morgan hoped Sergeant. Mills would resist arrest, so Lieutenant Morgan would have a reason to rough him up. It wouldn't be excessive force. It would be pay back. Lieutenant Morgan was so pissed at what Sergeant Mills had done, he wanted to hit something.

CHAPTER 38

The two detectives saw that Sergeant Mills' silver colored Jeep Cherokee was parked in the driveway when the two detectives pulled into the area. Detective Chase and Detective Clark were in an unmarked light blue Ford Taurus. When the detectives drove by the house, they saw Sergeant Mills loading a very large suitcase into the back of the car. Unfortunately, Sergeant Mills recognized the car as one belonging to the Sparks Police detective unit. Sergeant Mills may have been corrupt, but he wasn't stupid. He realized the call from dispatch, and the detective unit showing up, equaled they figured out he was a suspect in the gassing of dispatch, and the robberies that occurred at the two casinos and both banks.

Sergeant Mills ran into the house. The detectives knew they had been made. The detectives definitely knew this was not good. Detective Clark radioed to dispatch, asking Lieutenant Morgan to call them immediately. When Lieutenant Morgan called, he was told the surveillance was now a barricaded suspect. Lieutenant Morgan requested the Sparks SWAT Team respond.

Rob was notified via radio, that the Sparks and Reno SWAT Teams had been called out and were now mobilizing. The Command Post was in the parking lot of the Sparks Police Department. A Hostage Negotiator was called out since Sergeant Mills was not answering the land line or the cell phone. When Rob arrived, he saw that both Reno and Sparks Fire Departments were in the parking lot of the Sparks Police Department. He knew they were waiting for either the go ahead, or for the hazmat team to neutralize the gas. They were also waiting to hear if any hazardous materials were found in or around Sergeant Mills' house.

The firemen, when finding out that Sergeant Mills was a suspect in the gassing of the dispatch center, located in the basement of Reno Fire Station One, were heard making rude comments about where Sergeant Mills could put the gas. Rob knew that the police officers and deputies were very upset about their dispatchers, but Rob forgot that the firemen were equally upset. It was good that the firemen were on scene to assist with bringing the suspect into custody. The fire department would help in closing one of the biggest cases in Reno's history. Everyone wanted to storm the house and take Sergeant Mills into custody. They all felt that Sergeant Mills was getting everything he deserved. The only thing holding them back was the question, was he alone in his house?

Jim Gant, the Hostage Negotiator, tried for two hours calling Mark Mills. After getting no response on either the land line or the cell phones, he notified the SWAT Commander. SWAT Commander Judy Hoskins had team members sneak up to the house. The door and windows to the back of the house were all closed and locked.

They snuck around to the garage and found that the door was ajar. The SWAT Commander had been inside the house a Page couple of months before when Sergeant Mills, and his wife Beverly, had a barbecue for both Reno and Sparks Personnel. She remembered the garage door led into the kitchen. The kitchen led into the dining room.

Commander Hoskins also remembered it was an open floor plan. Commander Hoskins told SWAT Officer Lyman to look into the kitchen. He would have a clear view into that part of the house.

When SWAT Officer Lyman looked, he could not believe what he saw. There was a body hanging from the chandelier. SWAT Officer Lyman and Officer Adams slowly and silently backed out of the garage and reported the information to Commander Hoskins.

Commander Hoskins ordered the SWAT Team to enter the residence and clear each room, before the body was identified and removed. Each room was then searched and cleared. The officers only found two cats hiding and hissing under the bed in the master bedroom. When they checked the closets in the master bedroom and spare bedrooms, they found only men's clothing.

Apparently Beverly Mills had moved out of the house. FIS (Field Investigative Services) was called and had to be on scene before the body was cut down. Rob had promised the chief that everything would be done by the book. The body sounded like it was Mark Mills, but Rob was not taking any chances.

CHAPTER 39

It was a caucasian male, in his late 40s or early 50s. When Rob entered the house, he identified the body as Mark Mills. It appeared that Sergeant Mills had committed suicide, by hanging himself. Rob thought "that figures. Only a coward would take a way out that he did not have to be held accountable for what he did." Rob found a typed suicide not on the lap top computer. The computer was on the dining room table near where Sergeant Mills had hung himself.

The note indicated that Mark Mills was the mastermind behind all the incidents that occurred in Reno. It also indicated that he had gambled away all $2,000,000.

Rob thought, "is it finally over?" Rob thought it had been like trying to get rid of cock roaches. One usually escaped from the exterminator, to torment you again. But then Rob thought "this was too easy." The suicide could really be a homicide in disguise.

Because the suicide had occurred in Sparks Police's jurisdiction, the Sparks Police Department was going to investigate. Rob was glad to have them take it. Rob had his hands full pulling all the ends together on the case he had.

CHAPTER 40

Rob returned to the hospital to check on Caryn. Caryn had been napping and she looked better. Rob was thankful that Caryn was going to be okay. But, when Rob had asked Caryn earlier if she knew who had done this, she closed her eyes and sat very still. After a few minutes Rob thought she had fallen asleep. Caryn very softly said "I'm not getting anything." She said "Oh God, Rob, what did that stuff do to me? I never appreciated my ability before. I never saw it as a gift. But it's gone and I miss it. I don't feel like I'm me." This time when Rob reached for Caryn's hand, she opened her eyes and smiled. Rob kissed her and could not stop smiling at her. Caryn told Rob she just woke up a few minutes ago. Rob asked Caryn if she had talked to any of the nurses or doctors. Caryn told Rob she knew she was in a hospital, but she had not talked to anyone yet. Rob told Caryn "I have good news and I have bad news. Which one do you want to hear first?" Caryn couldn't help but smile. Caryn remembered Rob telling her just a few days ago, the same thing.

They were talking about Caryn's cat, Trouble. Rob told Caryn that he had been taking a nap while Caryn was shopping. Rob had just fallen asleep when Trouble jumped on his head. Rob told Caryn, "the good news was, your cat became a pilot." When Caryn asked for the bad news he said "your cat had a crash landing." Then Rob explained what had happened. When Rob pushed the cat off his head, the cat was jumping off the bed at the same time as Rob was pushing him. The cat flew off the bed and landed on the vanity bench. The cat turned around, gave Rob a dirty look and walked out.

Caryn figured Rob would tell her something funny now, so she asked for the bad news first. Rob said "honey, Carla, her boyfriend, his brother, and his friends set off a gas that got into the dispatch center. It knocked all of you out. The doctors are not hopeful for any recovery for Carla. They not only knocked out the other dispatchers and used the same gas on two casinos, killing a total of eighty-one people. They murdered seventy-eight who were elderly, had breathing problems, or were allergic to the gas. Three others just died from complications. The remaining victims are still recovering."

Caryn could not take in what Rob had said. Granted, Caryn had not gotten along with Carla. Carla could be a bitch. Carla was always yelling at someone. Sometimes she yelled at the police officers. Sometimes she yelled at the firemen. She almost got fired when she yelled at a hysterical woman to "shut the fuck up²' when Carla was trying to get information from her, after the woman had been beaten by her husband. For that, she got what amounted to a slap on the hand. Carla was suspended without pay for three days, and transferred to the graveyard shift. Caryn felt Carla was not the right type of person for a dispatching position. It took a special person who could handle an emergency the same way they handled a non-emergency. Calmly and professionally. Carla did not have that ability. Caryn thought she never would. Poor Carla.

Caryn was definitely ready to hear good news, so she asked Rob what the good news was. Rob couldn't help smiling from ear to ear. Rob leaned down and kissed Caryn. Then he leaned over and kissed Caryn's stomach. He looked at her and said "the good news is a miracle, our own little miracle." Then he got tears in his eyes and said "I love you so much, you are my life. I thought I would die when I was told you were unconscious, possibly dead. When the doctor told me you would be okay, that was my very own miracle. Our miracle is that we will be parents in about seven months. Honey, your about eight weeks pregnant.."

Caryn just looked at him. Rob realized the news finally sank in when he saw tears in her eyes. She softly said "a baby? I'm having a baby?" All Rob could do was nod. Then Caryn asked "is the baby all right? The gas did not affect the baby?" Rob told her what the doctors had said. Caryn could barely keep her eyes open but before she fell asleep she whispered to Rob thank you for being my husband, for giving me back my life. And, for a baby that I will love and cherish forever because the baby is the best part of both of us. I love you so much." Caryn then closed her eyes and fell asleep with her hands resting over her stomach, protecting the little life just forming inside.

CHAPTER 41

R ob went back to the station to report to the Chief
Williams. Rob told the chief that Caryn was awake. He
also excitedly told Chief Williams that he was going to be
a father. The chief said this calls for a celebration. Rob had
called him from Mark Mills house and told him that Sergeant
Mills was dead. Then Rob told Chief Williams it looked
like a suicide but Rob had an uneasy feeling about it. Rob
had a suspicion that Mark Mills had not taken his own life.
Someone may have taken it instead. The Chief asked Rob to
respond to the Coroner's Office. The Chief called in a favor
and asked that the autopsy be done as soon as possible.
When Rob arrived, the Medical Examiner was taking a blood
sample from Mark Mills, to check for any infectious diseases
that could be in the blood, and that would be a concern during the autopsy.

One routine test that was done was to check for HIV.
The test showed it was positive. Rob wondered if Mark knew
he was HIV positive. Did Mark have full blown AIDS? Rob
knew that anyone that was HIV positive was monitored by
the health department. If Rob was right, was the person Rob
suspected of killing Mark Mills also HIV positive? Was that
the reason Mark was murdered? Or was there another reason. Rob contacted the Washoe County Health Department.

Steve Fields, the Health Department Coordinator, told Rob that Mark Mills had been diagnosed approximately 6 years ago as having HIV. Did Beverly, Mark's widow know? That meant that Sally, Rob's ex-wife had been exposed too. Did Sally know she may be HIV positive?

Rob knew that not everyone HIV positive got AIDS. Later, the Medical Examiner told Rob that Mark Mills had AIDS when he died, and he wouldn't have lived much longer. Rob thought about what a pompous ass Mark Mills had been. Mark thought he could get away with the robberies and murders. Mark Mills probably knew this was his last chance to be the Chief of Police before he died. But was that why he committed suicide? But then Rob got one of his questions answered. The Medical Examiner told Rob "he didn't commit suicide, he was murdered. The eyes show he was smothered to death. He was hung to make it look like a suicide." Rob called Sparks Police Lieutenant Morgan and gave him the information. Lieutenant Morgan and Rob both agreed that the murder of Mark Mills was probably related to the incidents in Reno. Rob said he would take over the investigation of the death of Mark Mills and would keep Lieutenant Morgan apprised of all information. Rob got another surprise. Field Investigative Services Officer (FIS), Marla Watkins, told Rob that she found a fingerprint on the chair leg at Mark Mills' House. Marla told him the chair had been wiped down, but because it was found on the bottom of the seat near one of the legs, the suspect missed it. Rob was shocked to find out that the fingerprint came back to Rob's ex-wife, Sally.

Rob knew that Sally had left the Reno Police Department Dispatch Center after Mark and her had broken up. And after Rob and Caryn had gotten married. Rob had to find out where she went. Rob called the City of Reno Human

Resources Department. Since Sally had been a Dispatch Supervisor when she left, maybe she left a forwarding address with them.

Rob found out that Sally took a job with the Placer County Sheriff's Department. She was living near Lake Tahoe, in Tahoe City, California.

Rob thought that Sally was probably getting rid of all the loose ends. Rob had to get Sally before she left and disappeared. Rob knew Sally was smart and had an evil streak in her. But Rob had no idea she would turn out to be this evil. Rob contacted the Watch Commander at the Washoe County Sheriff's Department and asked to use their helicopter "Falcon." He asked to be picked up at the Reno Police Department. Rob knew he had to get to Sally as soon as possible. Rob was afraid that was time was running out. He did not want to call Placer County Sheriff's Department ahead of time, afraid that Sally would be tipped off that he was enroute to contact her. But because he was on official business, and as a department to department courtesy, he called the Watch Commander of Placer County Sheriff's Department. He notified them by phone. He asked the watch commander to keep their conversation confidential. Rob did not know how many friends or acquaintances Sally had at the Placer County Sheriff's Department. Rob knew if it was like the Reno Police Department, everyone that worked there felt they were part of a large family. If someone was in trouble, there were several people with the department, who would help them out. Luckily the watch commander agreed with Rob to keep the phone call confidential.

Falcon's crew radioed in that they had to stop for fuel before they picked up Rob. The helicopter landing pad was on the roof of the police station. When they arrived at the police station Rob was waiting for them. Rob got into the helicopter. He explained to the pilot, and the observer, that he had assigned a detective unit to respond to Placer County Sheriff's Department located on the South Shore of Lake Tahoe. The detective unit was responding in their department vehicle. Rob would only need Falcon to fly him to the South Shore of Lake Tahoe. They did not need to stand by. Rob had made arrangements for a deputy sheriff from Placer County to pick him up and take him to the Sheriff's Department. Rob told them he was en-route to interview and arrest a suspect in the "gassing" of the dispatchers. Also a suspect in the murders and robberies of the casinos and the banks. Rob didn't tell them she was a former Dispatch Supervisor for the City of Reno. He certainly wasn't going to tell them she was his ex-wife. After leaving the station, they started flying towards Lake Tahoe. Rob knew that Placer County Sheriff's Department handled all law enforcement needs of anyone on the California side of Lake Tahoe.

Lake Tahoe is a beautiful lake. It is called the eighth wonder of the world because of the beautiful scenery and clear water. Lake Tahoe is reported to be bottomless. It even has it's own lake monster, "Nessie." The lake is on the Nevada and California border. There are large casinos located on the Nevada side. Anyone visiting the casinos can gamble at the slot machines, poker tables, black jack tables, craps tables, keno, and other games. They can also stay at one of the luxury hotel rooms at any of the casinos. People visiting the lake have a variety of pastimes. Besides gambling, during the summer there is boating, swimming, or driving to the other side of the Lake into California. While in California, they may purchase lottery tickets. During the snowy winter months there is skiing and snow boarding. There are many specialty shops around Lake Tahoe where anyone can buy almost anything. The scenery is breathtaking, but visitors need to be aware of the altitude. It is high, and people have to become acclimated before performing any physical activities.

CHAPTER 42

Joe Zerloff, the observer, asked Rob if he wanted him to stow his duffel bag. Rob had not brought a duffel bag with him and told Joe that. All he had brought with him was a search warrant of Sally's house, her locker at the Sheriff's Department, and her vehicle. If Rob found what he expected to find, then he would arrest Sally for multiple charges includingmultiple murders. Rob saw there was a green duffel bag sitting between the seats. Rob told Joe that the bag did not belong to him. Joe checked with Mike Houston, the pilot, and found it wasn't his either. Joe asked Mike, "what should I do?" Mike said, "just like any airplane, any suspicious bags are to be checked thoroughly! "Rob knew that all baggage in airports were x-rayed. Oh how Rob wished for a portable x-ray machine right now.

Mike told Joe to look on the bag to see if there were any tags, or heaven help them, wires. Joe found a small piece of paper attached to the handle. It said, "To: Rob Stevens

Rob had not told anyone he was flying in the Falcon. Even Caryn did not know. Who could have left this package for him? And more important, what was in it? Rob zipped open the duffel bag very carefully. There was an white envelope inside. Under it was what appeared to be a vibrator, shaped like a very large dildo. Rob carefully picked up the envelope holding it by the edges. He could see it was unsealed and there was a note inside it. He was able to extract the note from the envelope. He was surprised to read:

Dear Rob,

knew the time would come when I would hear from you. I just wish it was under different circumstances. I know if your reading this, your on your way to arrest me. Your traveling at the fastest speed, which is in the helicopter. I'm going to save you some time. I'm not in California. I won't tell you where I am. I may have done some bad things, but I'm not stupid. After I took care of Mark Mills, I left for a much needed vacation. Heaven knows I deserved it after putting up with Mark'scrap for years. I'm at a place you cannot get an extradition warrant for my arrest. I took the $2,500,000. (that's right, 2.5 million). We got more money than anyone suspected. Gary was wrong about the amount.

I'm on an extended vacation forever.

With Love,

Sally

P.S. To get your attention, the dildo in the bag is a pipe bomb. I suggest you don't touch it. The dildo reminded me of Mark, because he was such a prick.

P.P.S. Don't panic. It's not connected. I just wanted you to remember me.

CHAPTER 43

I YEAR LATER

Lieutenant Rob Stevens was baby-sitting. His son, John Robert Stevens, was sleeping peacefully. J.R. (the nickname they gave their son) had just turned 5 months old. Caryn had fully recuperated. All of the dispatchers had recovered, except one. Carla never woke up. The doctors told Rob she was in a vegetative state and would probably never recover. Rob felt that Carla suffered more than Gary, Tommy, or the rest of their gang.

Carla's parents, Joe and Jill Anderson, could not believe their little girl could have had anything to do.with what happened in Reno. Joe and Jill had lived in Truckee, California, all their lives. They liked the small town size. Truckee, California, was a laid back community which was located in the Sierra Mountains, west of Reno.

During the time Carla was growing up, Jill would go shopping in Reno, once a week, since most of the stores in Truckee were tourist shops. The shops in Truckee sold things like cold weather clothing for the cold winter months. They also had shops that sold souveneirs, jewelry and antiques. Most of the citizens of Truckee would go to Reno, since there was a larger selection of products, and most of the stores in Truckee were novelty shops. Jill liked going to Reno, but was even happier when she came home. Jill was just a small town girl.

When Carla went with Jill, Carla always begged her mom to stay in Reno for just a few hours more. Carla would want to go to dinner and a movie. Granted, there were restaurants in Truckee, but Carla loved the bright lights of the big city. Joe was very strict and insisted "both my girls" be back before dinner. Joe wanted nothing to do with Reno, Nevada. At one time Joe had gotten lost in Reno, been mugged in Reno, and lost all his money in a casino in Reno. As far as Joe was concerned, Reno, Nevada was evil and Joe wanted nothing to do with it. It was okay for Jill to go shopping there, but he liked her to return home before it got dark. Joe just felt that worse things happened in Reno, Nevada, after dark.

When his daughter, Carla, moved to Reno, Joe felt Carla had made a big mistake. When Carla started working for the City of Reno, Joe thought "maybe I'mwrong about Reno." Joe was very proud of his daughter and told all his friends and neighbors about Carla being a dispatcher for the Reno Police Department. Joe would tell them she would be running the place in a few years. Joe was starting to think, "Reno's not all bad. Maybe I was wrong about it."

When the attack on dispatch was headline news on the morning news show in Truckee, California, several friends and neighbors rushed to Joe and Jill's house. They not only responded to stand by their side, they brought food to sustain them through their time of need. After all, in a small town everyone shared the ups and downs of life, with their friends and neighbors.

Jill cried just thinking about "those poor people", and not only the dispatchers, but the ones that were in the casinos when they were attacked. Joe kept thinking "I knew it. It just proves Reno is evil."

When the phone call came in later that morning, it was Chief Bill Williams. Bill told Joe , on behalf of the City of Reno Police Department, how sorry he was. Joe could not believe what he was hearing. One of the dispatchers that had been attacked was his daughter, Carla. Joe thanked the chief, and hung up. When he turned around to face all the expectant friends that were watching him, Joe had tears in his eyes. Jill screamed. She thought Joe was going to tell her that Carla had died, like some of the others that had been attacked. Joe rushed to her side and kept repeating, "Carla is alive, Carla is alive." Jill said "thank you God." Joe explained to everyone that Carla had been injured. She was one of the dispatchers that had been attacked. She was being taken to the hospital. That's all Joe knew. That's all Chief Williams had told him.

After Joe and Jill had arrived at the hospital, and after talking to the doctor, Joe was devastated to learn his daughter was in a coma. When Joe then learned that the other dispatchers who had been with Carla, were waking up, Joe sat by Carla's side waiting for her to do the same. Jill and Joe would talk to Carla as if she was awake and listening to them. But Carla never gave them any indication that she ever heard them.

Tommy, Gary, and the others never actually admitted that Carla was a suspect, or involved. When Tommy told Rob everything that had happened, he said Carla never knew what they had planned. Rob knew Tommy lied, but Rob felt that Carla had suffered enough. Carla was in her own prison, serving out her sentence.

After a couple of weeks, with no improvement, the doctors agreed to release Carla into Joe and Jill's care. With the help of the friends and neighbors, Carla received the care she required, even though she never regained consciousness.

Tommy would faithfully write a letter, every week, to Carla. Tommy always started the letter out apologizing. Then he would write how much he loved her. Tommy wasn't sure if her parents ever read the letters to her. Joe would always intercept the letter and tear it up. Sometimes he would burn it. He never opened them, to read them. Joe never told Jill about the letters. Joe was sure that the only reason his daughter was like this, was because of Tommy and his brother, Gary.

When Tommy was arrested he was placed under "suicide watch." Rob thought Tommy might try to kill himself. Tommy screamed and cried, asking to talk to Carla. Rob repeated over and over that no one could talk to Carla. Carla was in a coma, and the doctors told Rob that if she had not recovered by this time, chances were her chance of recovery was very slim. Tommy just asked to see Carla. While Rob was transporting Tommy to jail, Rob took a shortcut and stopped by the hospital.

Rob knew he did not owe Tommy anything. After all, he was one of them. He had put Rob's beautiful wife and child in jeopardy. But Rob was hoping that once Tommy saw Carla, he would give Rob all the information he needed. Rob also knew, if it was Caryn instead of Carla laying there, Rob would be so depressed he wouldn't know what to do with himself. Rob wasn't sure if he would go on a rampage, and all the suspects would end up dead or dying, saving the state the cost of a trial and extended time in prison. Or, would Rob just sit at Caryn's side, not caring about anything but watching over Caryn. Would he be so heart broken that he could not do his job. Rob felt sorry for Tommy in that Tommy was not allowed to have a short visit with Carla. Carla would not even know Tommy was there. When they arrived, Tommy apologized to Carla. He kept begging Carla to open her eyes. Tommy finally broke down into hysterical sobs. Tommy looked at Rob and said, "I've lost everything important in my life. I have nothing left." Rob took Tommy to jail and placed him under suicide watch. Rob felt in that respect, Tommy and Rob were both alike. They loved their woman with all their heart, and could not live without her in their life.

When Gary asked to see his brother Tommy, Tommy refused saying unemotionally, "I have no brother." Gary yelled and screamed, hoping Tommy could, or would hear him. Gary hoped that Tommy knew he would never have hurt Carla on purpose. Gary knew that Tommy adored Carla. Gary just hoped that some day Tommy would forgive him. Gary kept hoping that the someday would be today.

At the trial, Tommy, Gary and the others all stood trial at the same time. Since the charges were the same, the prosecuting attorney, and the defense attorneys all agreed that it would save time and money. The charges were unbelievable. 110 counts of murder in the first degree. The weapon used in the murders was the gas that was used to immobilize the victims. 102 charges of attempted murder. Again, the weapon used was the gas that immobilized the victims. 2 charges of bank robbery. The weapon used was a vehicle and the dynamite they used to crack open the safes. And the last charge was terrorism. They jeopardized the lives of an entire community by disabling the 911 emergency system. They disabled the dispatchers that were working that morning. They disabled the people and took away their ability, for any calls to be received to the police departments, sheriff's department, or the fire department, via the dispatch center.

All of the prisoners, except one, pleaded "not guilty." Tommy was the one that pleaded guilty. Tommy said he hurt the very last person in the world that he could imagine hurting. Carla was his love. Carla was his heart. Carla would never be the same person she had been before she met him. And for that, he was indeed guilty. Tommy was sentenced to life in prison, with parole possible after he had served eighty years. Everyone knew, even Tommy, that he would never leave prison alive. He would never be free. Tommy felt it was only right since Carla was in a prison of her own. And,

Tommy had put her there. Tommy knew if his brother, Gary, had not talked him into involving Carla, she may not have been affected the way she was. Tommy kept blaming himself. Tommy never thought that Carla should share in the blame. Tommy never thought about the fact that no one had forced Carla to become involved in the crimes committed. Carla only thought about the money she would have gotten.

Tommy was sentenced to serve his time at the Lovelock State Prison in Nevada. When Gary was convicted (did anyone think he wouldn't be), Gary was also sentenced to the Lovelock State Prison in Nevada. Gary was hoping to see Tommy. Gary felt if he had to, he would beg Tommy to forgive him. Gary thought, "he can't ignore me forever." As far as Rob knew, as of today, Tommy refused to see his brother, much less have any sort of conversation.

Rob thought about Sally. How he had lived with her for years, and never knowing that she was capable of murder. She had murdered Mark Mills. The worse part was, she had never had to answer for all the pain and destruction she had caused. Gary, Tommy and his gang of thugs were serving terms of life in prison with no chance for parole. Rob knew that Gary and Tommy were both at the Lovelock Prison, but Rob wasn't sure of where the others were.

CHAPTER 44

Caryn was having dinner with friends. Caryn and Rob had decided, just before J.R. was born, each one of them would take a night away. Both Rob and Caryn knew that life was too short not to live it to the fullest, every day. They decided they could do whatever they wanted to do, while the other one babysat. Rob enjoyed spending time bonding with his son. They both loved being together, but they both knew that a little time apart was good for them. After all, it was usually only 4 or 5 hours. Neither one wanted to stay apart longer than that. Caryn was meeting with some other dispatchers that were just getting off work, or had the day off. Caryn hadn't gone back to work since she was still on maternity leave.

The doctors did not know what the side effects to the drug were going to be. Caryn and the other dispatchers who worked with her that night, were closely monitored. They had standing appointments once a week, unless there was a health issue. Then they would go in more often. If they felt ill, then they went in immediately. So far there were no side effects. The doctor suggested that Caryn stay on maternity leave until J.R. was 1 year old. Rob didn't mind having Caryn home. Rob didn't think Caryn minded either.

Rob had just sat down to enjoy his nightly cup of coffee, after placing a very tired J.R. in his crib. The doorbell rang.

Rob rushed to the door, afraid that whoever was at the door would ring the bell again, waking up J.R. When Rob looked through the peep hole in the door, he saw a delivery man. The man was pushing a cart containing a very large box. Rob knew Caryn ordered books sometimes. It could be a new shipment. Caryn was an avid reader and Rob could not help but laugh at theirgrowing library. Rob didn't think that Caryn had ordered that many books but who knew? The box looked like it could contain at least 2 dozen books. Rob had to sign for the package and was surprised it was addressed to him and not Caryn. No return address was listed. Rob, with the help of the delivery driver, dragged the box into the house. The box was not as heavy as it looked, but it was quite large and bulky.

Rob carefully opened the box after making sure the delivery man had left in his truck. Rob could not believe what he was looking at. There was a plain white envelope sitting on top of what Rob considered a shit load of money. Rob opened the envelope, and was surprised to see it was from Sally.

He read:

Dear Rob,

I bet your shocked to hear from me. When you read this I will be dead. I not only got $2,500,000. from that prick Mark, I also got AIDS. I spent as much money as I could, before my health got so bad. I thought about returning the money to the banks and casinos, but I worked too hard to get it. The banks and casinos are insured any ways. They have probably already collected their insurance money. Then I thought of you. You put up with me for a long time. You put up with a lot of shit over the years. And since I was your ex-wife, the police department may have suspected you were also involved. I'm sorry if that happened. I never planned to have anyone know I was involved. I was going to take vacation time from work, and never return. I sent all the money that was left, to you. You can do with it what you want. I did not expect it to end this way. I hope you have a good life. Say hello to Caryn for me. It was signed simply "Sally."

Rob sat there and just looked at the box containing all that money. The money was in mostly $100.00 bills. And there were a lot of those. Rob started counting and put the $100's into bundles of $5,000. He had 350 bundles, totaling $1,750,000. just in hundreds. He counted the twenties and put them in bundles of a $1,000.

He ended up with 5 bundles adding up to $5,000. With this the grand total was $1,755,000.

Rob was stunned. Rob remembered, for the longest time there were rumors that Sally was seen, shopping in resorts all over the World. But, none of the sightings had been confirmed. Rob always thought that Sally was somewhere, laughing her ass off, spending the money like there was no tomorrow. Everyone, even Rob, thought all the money was gone. They thought Sally took it and was never coming back. It looked like they were right about Sally never coming back. Rob never thought it would be because Sally had died. That had never crossed his mind. Rob did not know what he should do, but he knew what he wanted to do. He wanted to give some of the money to local charities and to help the homeless. He wanted to spend some of it on Caryn and J.R. He never wanted to worry about money again. He wanted to go on a nice vacation. He also wanted to buy everything Caryn and him had ever talked about. Should he do the ethical thing and turn it in? Or, should he do the moral thing and help all the people he would be able to help. After all, he could help the people of Reno that had been affected by what Sally, Carla, Mark, Gary, Tommy and the rest of them, had done.

Rob thought, I'll think about it. I'm not going to rush. No one knows Sally sent the money to her ex-husband. I'll make my decision tomorrow, after I have a good night's sleep, and think about it a little more. When he got up the next morning, Rob knew what he needed to do.

CHAPTER 45

7 MONTHS LATER

Caryn went back to work. Caryn had not only recovered, but her psychic abilities came back stronger than ever. Caryn and Rob still tried to keep her psychic abilities a secret. Jack would sometimes stop by. He was now the Commander of Investigations. He was still still Rob's supervisor, but also a good friend to both Caryn and Rob. He was also J.R.'s godfather. When he came by, he usually brought a file with him. It was usually a case where the police department had hit a dead end, then hitting a brick wall. Caryn would look at the file for a few minutes. Months before, she had explained to Jack that sometimes she would get a feeling where she had to look at something closer. It might be a person, or a certain area of the report. After Tom's kidnapping, Caryn tried to keep her field work at a minimum. But Tom was alive and well, Thank God. Sometimes what Caryn was seeing, or feeling was so strong that she would have Rob or Jack take her where she "needed" to go. Jack totally believed in Caryn's ability. He hadn't wanted to, but hecould not deny what Caryn was able to do. Jack sometimes felt bad, when he received the recognition for a job well done, when he would not have done it without Caryn's help. He also knew that Caryn did not want to bring attention to herself. When Jack would mention that Caryn should get the recognition she deserved, she would tell him "if you hadn't believed Rob, and believed in me, we all would have suffered in the end." Jack understood what she said, but sometimes felt it wasn't always that easy. After all, Jack now had to believe in something he could not see, could not touch or feel. Jack thought to himself, "does anyone know how tough that is?"

Ron was promoted to lieutenant and assigned to the traffic division. Ron had enjoyed working patrol. He thought he was sure he was going to be bored silly. Or, buried under a lot of paperwork that would take forever to dig out from underneath. Ron was surprised when he found out his new position gave him something that he thought he had lost a long time ago. Satisfaction in a job well done. When Rob worked as a patrol sergeant, he would begin an investigation, but either the next shift coming on would continue with what Ron started. Or, the patrol lieutenant would call detectives, and have an investigator take over. Now, as lieutenant of traffic, Ron would have the last say in all accident investigations. From the little "fender benders", to the fatality accidents. From the D.U.I. that drives into a parked car, to the hit and runs. Ron enjoyed the challenge. Surprisingly, Ron would visit Caryn occasionally, to ask for help. He enjoyed their visits. He could never forget what Caryn was capable of. He remembered the last time he needed herspecial expertise. It was just before last Christmas. It had snowed a little. Just enough snow to make the streets slushy, and make them look very dirty. But it hadn't gotten slick yet. It was early evening. Ron had heard the radio call being dispatched, when Ron was driving his police department assigned car. Ron had just left the police station, headed for home. Ron remembered it being about 5:30 P.M. Ron had spent all that day signing off on reports that he had reviewed. Ron had the utmost respect for all of the officers, but the traffic division was a specialized division of the police department. The officers only handled traffic accidents, and/or writing traffic tickets. Ron was afraid some of the officers assigned traffic division would become bored. And, maybe make stupid mistakes because the reports were repetitious. But Ron found all of the officers to be dedicated, hardworking officers, and they understood that a hit and run accident was just as devastating to the victim. It was like the victim had been assaulted or burglarized. The victim felt defiled. The victim felt desperate. An unknown suspect had hurt "their baby", their "pride and joy." The traffic officers took their job very seriously, just like every officer, no matter what division they were assigned to. The officers never believed a minor accident was "that minor." Not until the investigation had been completed. Most of the time the accident was just what it was, an accident. Sometimes it was no one's fault. The sun was shining in the windshield, blinding the driver, or a dog ran into the roadway, causing the driver to swerve into on coming traffic.

Ron heard the dispatcher send a traffic unit and two patrol units to a hit and run, possible fatality. Ron radioed that he was also enroute. When he arrived at 5th Street and Kirman, he got out of his vehicle to investigate. All three officers had arrived, along with a fire engine and an ambulance. Ron knew that the area of 5th Street and Kirman was not in a very good area of the City of Reno. The police department had waged war with the gang bangers and the drug pushers, for as long as Ron could remember. Every time they cleaned up the area, it was only a matter of weeks before it needed to be cleaned up again. Unfortunately, it took a lot of man power from the police department to do that. What with the budget cut backs for the police department, the first program to go was the

"Neighborhood Renewal Program." Even with four police cars, a fire engine and an ambulance on scene, Ron was not surprised to notice no one standing in front of their house wondering "what happened." Ron knew their attitude was "I didn't see anything, I didn't hear anything, I don't know anything."

Ron walked up to one of the officers and asked him "what happened." The officer explained they had received an anonymous call into dispatch, about two people lay-ing in the middle of the street. The call taker said the caller sounded intoxicated. He told the call taker he did not know what had happened. He just drove by and saw them in the street. Since he hadn't seen anything, he did not want to get involved. Then he hung up. The officer told Ron that the firemen had arrived first. They had radioed in that they had two people down. It appeared that both people were victims of a hit and run. Shortly after that, the firemen told their dispatcher that both subjects were "code 50."

When the first officer arrived, he noticed what appeared to be "tread marks" on the victim's clothing. It appeared that the male victim's head had been the only part of his body that had been run over. Ron hoped they found some identification in his pocket, or that his prints were on file. Because when Ron saw the male victim, he knew that no one was going to able to identify him by looking at him. He was unrecognizable. The female victim had been a little luckier, if you call being run over and killed by a vehicle, lucky. Both her legs had been run over, but her face and head were left unscathed. When the coroner arrived, he searched both bodies and could not find any identification on either one of them. Ron later learned that neither the male, nor the females fingerprints were on file.

The autopsy determined they had both died before they had been run over. They both died of drug overdoses. Ron turned the investigation over to the drug enforcement investigators, since it was no longer considered a hit and run. But, Ron never forgot them. Ron would see the female's face on the news or in the newspaper, asking for anyone who knew her to call the Reno Police Department. Lots of people called in, but the calls never panned out. Both the male and female remained unidentified.

Ron decided to stop by and visit Caryn. Ron could not get those two people out of his mind. He usually considered drug users as people who knew the risk. If they died, it was their own fault. But Ron felt there was more to this story. When Ron saw Caryn, Caryn told Ron to check with Circus Circus Casino Lost and Found. Caryn told Ron she had a feeling that some of your questions would be answered there. When Ron arrived at Circus Circus Casino, he explained to the lost and found supervisor what he was doing there. He told her he was trying to identify two people. He told her he had received an anonymous tip that the two people could be identified here. Sandy, from lost and found, brought out the identification cards and drivers licenses that had been left behind within the past year. To Ron it looked like there were at least a hundred of them. Ron then asked Sandy if some of the identification had been found at the same time, in the same room. Ron thought if both subjects forgot their I.D., they may have been found together. After Sandy checked her files, she placed 6 identification cards and/or drivers licenses in three stacks. She put those stacks in front of Ron. The second stack contained what Ron had been searching for. Both

I.D's showed that the two victims were from California. They had been attending the University of California, in Berkley.

Ron called Sgt. Lee Farber with the Drug Enforcement Divison. Lee thanked Rob for the information. Lee called Ron the following day to tell him what he found out. He told Ron it turned out both subjects were in the Reno area to visit the boy's family. Jim Wilson and his girlfriend, Samantha Fancher, had come to visit Jim's cousin, Frank Mueller. Turned out that Frank was a meth user. While Frank was tripping on meth, he dared Jim and Samantha to try it too. Lee told Ron, after Jim and Samantha accepted the dare, they both walked outside to look at the "freaking stars that were talking to them." Because of the amount of drugs, and the altitude, and the lack of sleep after mid terms, their hearts just could not take it. Their hearts simply stopped. They both died within minutes of each other. Lee also found out that the anonymous caller turned out to be the one that ran over them. The drunk driver had been released from jail, after being arrested for his third DUI. He decided to celebrate his release, by getting drunk and driving home.

Ron called Caryn and thanked her. Ron had needed to identify those two people, for his own peace of mind. He needed closure. Ron was thankful he was able to get back on track. Ron never tried to let his work come home with him, but before he identified both subjects, that case had haunted him. Ron felt that a huge weight had been lifted off him. Ron wasn't sure if Caryn knew how special she was, but he was sure Rob did.

CHAPTER 46

Caryn always told Rob that she enjoyed dispatching. But she never liked doing the work in the basement of the fire station. The only thing she enjoyed about being in the basement of the fire station was, she enjoyed visiting with the firemen, when they could stop by in dispatch. She enjoyed hearing their stories about the fires they put out, or the rescue they had completed successfully. But that was not enough for Caryn to want to return to the basement. Also because of the bad memories, and the thought that it could have turned out a lot worse. Now Caryn was excited about returning to work because it wasn't at the old dispatch center that had been located in the basement of the Fire Station. None of the dispatchers had felt comfortable in the basement, after the attack. They were always nervous thinking, "what if it happened again?" The dispatch staff decided to stay at the alternate dispatch center, that was located at the Washoe County Building. Unfortunately, there was not a lot of space, and not all of the equipment was hooked up. After all, the alternate dispatch center was supposed to be just temporary. The dispatch staff had asked the city councilmen, and City Manager John Foster to build a new dispatch center. A dispatch center that was above ground. The city manager told the councilmen, and the dispatchers that the city could not afford it. Several months after

Caryn, Linda and Mike had been released from the hospital, they were contacted by a well known Reno attorney. When Caryn and her fellow dispatchers had received the calls, he told them he had received a generous cash retainer from an anonymous donor. He was hired to sue the City of Reno if they did not move the dispatch center to another location. Somewhere safer, and out of the basement. The dispatchers were all excited. They hadn't felt comfortable in the basement for years. Some of the dispatchers even suspected there was mold behind the carpeting, that was on the walls of the room to keep the noise at a minimum.

The City Attorney met with the Chief of Police, the Fire Chief, the Mayor, and the City Manager. After some discussion, they all agreed it was better to keep the dispatchers safe. After all, they were the backbone to all the agencies they dispatched for. The City of Reno found out, the hard way, if there were no dispatchers, everything stops. No one is safe. The dispatchers are the ones that kept all the agencies up and running, and kept them up to date on all calls. They were the ones that were the middle men or middle women. They always worked between the agencies they dispatched for, and the public they assisted every day. They were very dedicated employees that did a difficult job. They did that job every day, to the best of their ability. They got the job done.

The homeless shelter was also enjoying a windfall. They received an anonymous cash donation of $250,000. That money would go a long way to feed and house the homeless. Already it was turning into a cold winter and the shelter usually had to cut corners. Now they had enough money to buy blankets, cots, not to mention food, to give to the number of people they knew would seek help.

Meanwhile, the local newspaper had done a story, spot lighting a family, once a week, for twenty weeks. All twenty families were having a difficult time to make ends meet. They were having financial difficulties for a multitude of reasons. These twenty families were also thankful.

The mother, or the father, or sometimes both, were working, but because of the cost of living they were falling further behind. The power company, or the gas company were getting ready to turn off their utilities. These twenty families found out that an anonymous donor had not only paid for their past due bills, but paid towards the next 6 months. This gave each of the families a chance to catch up on their other bills, and dig themselves out of their financial holes. The families wanted to thank the anonymous donor, but they found out the bills had been paid in cash. The power company explained that an envelope was received via the mail, with very explicit instructions.

The local newspaper had been writing about this anonymous hero for several days. The paper was hoping that someone knew who this person was. The editor had written several editorials praising this anonymous person. The editor, on behalf of everyone who was helped financially, wanted to thank whoever this person was. The editor was surprised when no one ever came forward or even said they knew who the person was.

CHAPTER 47

Rob was reading the daily newspaper. Rob was enjoying being on his days off. He now had the same days off that Caryn did. Rob enjoyed doing things as a family. Life was great. He also enjoyed reading about this anonymous person. He was glad that the person was in a position to help so many people. In Rob's line of work, Rob saw a lot of people every day. There were so many people out there that needed help. Most of the time, the help they needed was just temporary. Until they could get back on their feet. Rob thought about the report he had read. It was about a woman who filed the burglary report. While she was helping an elderly neighbor, someone had broken into her apartment and had taken her only means of entertainment, her old black and white television set.

When Caryn came into the kitchen, Rob was sitting at the kitchen table, drinking his coffee and reading his newspaper. Rob turned to Caryn, pointed to the newspaper article he had been reading about the anonymous donor. He told Caryn, "I know someone who could use help from this wonderful anonymous person. Caryn smiled and said "I'll get right on it."

Rob smiled and said, "Caryn, you read my mind."

Made in the USA
Charleston, SC
27 October 2010